Margaret slipped the coins in… the satisfying jingle they made when they dropped inside.

"Well, that's not fair," Meli pouted. "I'm the one who noticed your bonnet first. If I had known you would part with it, I'd have offered you six."

Six dollars! Almost enough to pay room and board at Miss Priscilla's for two more weeks! "Meli, I don't want to see you disappointed. Do you like blue? I have a lovely blue satin bonnet that would just match your eyes. I could bring it to you tomorrow, if you'd like."

Meli's eyes lit up like a child who'd just seen a Christmas tree. "Oh, yes, yes! I do love blue. What time shall I meet you here tomorrow?"

"Let's come early before the sun gets too high," Margaret suggested. "How about nine o'clock?"

"I'll be here," Meli exclaimed. "Are you sure the blue one is just as pretty as Katherine's?"

"It's even prettier," Margaret promised. "That's why it's worth an extra dollar." She did not want to give Meli a chance to forget that she had promised to pay her six dollars.

This time the ladies let her pass through the door. As Margaret walked down the porch steps, she could hear the silver coins jingling in her reticule.

MUNCY G. CHAPMAN has four children who magically became eight (ie, their spouses), and then was blessed with eleven grandchildren. All live in Florida. She says she is married to the most wonderful man in the world with whom she recently celebrated their golden wedding anniversary. Muncy likes to sew, cook, play the piano, and of course, write. She works with the children in her church, and also with the shut-ins as a "Caring Caller." She enjoys writing with her husband. He likes the research and she likes choosing the words.

Books by Muncy G. Chapman

HEARTSONG PRESENTS
HP266—What Love Remembers

Margaret's Quest

Muncy G. Chapman

Heartsong Presents

For my girls: Jill, Margy, Melinda, and Kathy.

A note from the author:
*I love to hear from my readers! You may correspond with me
by writing:*   **Muncy G. Chapman**
                      Author Relations
                      PO Box 719
                      Uhrichsville, OH 44683

ISBN 1-57748-542-4

MARGARET'S QUEST

Cover illustration by Jocelyne Bouchard.

PRINTED IN THE U.S.A.

one

On a crisp February morning in 1836, Margaret Porter stood on the deck of the schooner *Windsong* and let the breeze have its way with her long, dark hair. Her full skirts billowed around her ankles and she used both hands to restrain them lest they rise to reveal the ruffles of her new lace pantelettes.

As a small child holding fast to her father's hand while he made his daily tour of the tobacco warehouses, she had stood on the Savannah docks many times and watched the schooners pass. But not even then, and not in her wildest dreams since, had she ever imagined that she would someday travel on a vessel like the magnificent *Windsong*.

She breathed deeply and filled her lungs with the salty air. Out here on the high sea, even the air smelled different from that which blew along the Savannah waterfront: fresher, cleaner—exhilarating!

A northeasterly wind filled the great, white sails above her head, puffing them out to resemble giant goose-down pillows. White-capped ocean swells slapped against the side of the schooner, causing it to pitch and roll, but contrary to her father's dire warnings, Margaret found the rocking motion most pleasant.

Her excitement was twofold. She would be traveling beyond the boundaries of the United States into the mysterious region known as the Florida Territory. But any fears that she might have entertained were quickly dispelled when she thought of the handsome fiancé who would be waiting there for her.

The moment she had laid eyes on Captain Allen Fairchild,

she had vowed that she would somehow manage an introduction. In all of her twenty years, she had never seen such a handsome man! He filled out his army uniform with broad, muscular shoulders, and sleek, black hair framed a finely chiseled face that seemed to wear a perpetual smile.

She was not ashamed of the way she had manipulated their introduction. In fact, she was rather proud of her clever ingenuity. She had just entered Marshall's Emporium that morning when she had seen him standing in front of the handkerchief counter. Without hesitation, she had grabbed up an armload of merchandise that she had no intention of purchasing—spools of thread, a bonnet, three skeins of yarn, and other items she did not even pause to identify—and moved across the floor in his direction. When she had drawn almost abreast of him, she'd positioned her bonnet so that it obstructed her view, and then she'd plowed headlong into his tall, unsuspecting frame.

Merchandise had flown out of her arms and scattered across the floor.

"Oh, I'm sorry, miss." The soldier had begun to apologize profusely for the "accident" that was in no way his fault. He'd stooped to gather the items from the floor, and she had bent to help him. In this odd position, their eyes had met and locked, and he'd dropped the yarn he had just retrieved. "S–sorry," he had stammered. "I'm not usually so clumsy!"

"Nor am I!" She'd stood and held out her hand. "I'm Margaret Porter. I'm afraid I wasn't watching where I was going."

He had taken her hand and had not released it right away. "I'm Allen Fairchild, and I'm very pleased to make your acquaintance, even under such unfavorable circumstances."

"Why, Mr. Fairchild, what a nice thing to say. Are you stationed here in Savannah?"

"No, but my parents live here. I'm just home for a short

furlough. I'll soon be going back to join the rest of my company at Fort Brooke."

"Is that in Georgia?"

Allen had laughed. "How I wish! No, it's way down south in the Florida Territory."

As they had talked, an aproned stock boy had begun to retrieve the merchandise and place it on the counter. Allen, whose eyes had never left Margaret's face, had said, "The least that I can do to make amends is to buy you a cup of tea. I'll wait while you complete your purchases, and then perhaps you will do me the honor of accompanying me to Miss Bessie's Tearoom."

Margaret had looked at the stack of randomly chosen merchandise piled neatly on the wooden counter. She had no use for any of it. "Oh, my, I'm afraid I'll have to come back later to finish my shopping," she had said, fluttering her eyelashes in a coquettish manner. "I do feel a little shaken, and a cup of tea might be just what I need to settle my nerves."

That contrived introduction was the beginning of their whirlwind courtship. Allen had asked permission to call on her, and for the rest of his leave, he had spent every possible hour in her company.

Margaret, who had never lacked for male attention, nevertheless found his obvious devotion both flattering and enjoyable. On the eve of his departure, he had proposed to her beneath the huge magnolia trees, where silver moonlight spread dancing shadows across her lawn. In breathless excitement, she had accepted, and the two of them had sealed their promise with a kiss.

Now scarcely three months later, Margaret stood on the deck of a giant schooner on her way to join him. Without the scent of magnolia blossoms or a moonlit sky, what, at the moment, had seemed so terribly romantic now seemed just a trifle awesome.

Her father had offered all kinds of objections to this journey, and most of them Margaret had to admit were valid. She had not known Allen long, and she knew very little about him. She only knew that the very thought of him sent her blood racing through her veins in a most exciting way and that her fondest dream was to become his wife. She was twenty years old already, and she certainly did not want to end up as a spinster! And handsome men like Allen Fairchild did not happen along every day.

She tried to picture what a handsome couple they would make walking down the streets of Tampa, she in one of her elegant new dresses, he in his regal military uniform. It bothered her just a little that she now had difficulty recalling his facial features—she had not seen him for three months—but she did remember that he was a very tall and strikingly handsome man, and she would be proud to stand beside him as his wife!

Her father had also pointed out that a more proper order of events would be for Allen to return to Savannah to marry his daughter before she set off alone on this long, dangerous journey to an unknown land. Although Margaret could not disagree, she knew that for Allen, such a move would be almost impossible. How could he come to Savannah for her when he was stationed so far away at Fort Brooke near Tampa? The United States Army did not give its soldiers vacations to pursue their personal interests, romantic or otherwise. Allen had explained all that to her and told her that they were in the midst of a fierce conflict with the Seminole Indians, forcibly moving them out of the Florida Territory to relocate in Oklahoma.

"The Indians are putting up a fierce resistance," he had told her. "They know their way around the woods and swamps of the territory much better than we do, and they're much better adapted to the tropical climate. I wish President

Jackson would just let them stay. After all, they were there before we were."

Margaret tried to explain this situation to her father, and she refused to accept his suggestion that she wait until Allen could come for her. That might be years away. Why, he might even meet and marry someone else before he was granted leave again. Margaret had heard about brazen women who followed the troops from post to post, and a man as handsome as Allen would be a prime target for their wiles.

Her only regrets now were the lack of her father's blessing and the bitter words that had passed between them. He had not even come to the docks to see her off. Would he ever forgive her for going against his wishes? She hoped that he would be able to in time.

She had written to Allen to tell him the name of the ship on which she would be arriving and the date of her departure. Her date of arrival would be dependent on weather conditions. She could only hope that he had received her letter and would be at the dock in Tampa to meet her. The mails were so slow; she had received only one letter from him since he left Savannah, and that he had written soon after his return to Fort Brooke.

"It's a bit brisk out here, miss. Wouldn't you like to go inside out of the wind?"

Margaret turned her head to see who had intruded into her daydreams. "No, I—" She looked up into eyes the color of the sea on a stormy day—dark, cobalt blue. The gentlemen was smiling at her in such a friendly manner that she could not remain angry with him for the interruption. She noted that he was very tall, and his hair, the color of fine corn silk, curled softly where it met the edge of his collar. "I—um—rather enjoy the ocean air," she finished.

"Well then, I'll leave you to your meditation. I'm Mikal Lee, part owner of this ship. We like to make sure that all of our passengers are comfortable, so if there is ever anything you need, please let one of us know."

"No, there is nothing. I mean, the ship is wonderful. I expected the ride to be much rougher. That is, I was told. . ."

"As long as we don't hit any bad weather, you should be able to enjoy your trip. A schooner this size generally rides easier than the smaller ones."

"Thank you, Captain Lee."

He grinned, revealing white, perfectly spaced teeth and an impish twinkle in his eyes. "Whoa, I'm not the captain. I'm just an ordinary guy. Please call me Mikal."

"All right, Mikal, and I'm Margaret—Margaret Porter. Anyway, thank you for your concern."

She offered her hand and he held it gently, as if it were a piece of fine silk.

"I apologize for interrupting your morning meditation, Margaret. You see, I come out here myself each day for my daily devotions, and I know how bothersome interruptions can be." He released her hand and turned to go, but called over his shoulder, "Good-bye, Margaret. I'll pray for your safe and pleasant journey."

How odd! Margaret thought as she watched him walk away. She had only just met him, and already he was offering to pray for her. And he seemed to think she was engaged in some sort of religious meditation. He couldn't have been farther from the truth! Although she had received Christian training as a child, she had pushed all that aside when she became an adult. She would prefer to manage her own life, thank you very much, and so far she was doing very well!

Still, there was something very intriguing about Mikal Lee. He was different from other men she had met, and she was just curious enough to want to learn more about him.

Margaret saw him several more times over the next few days, but he was always busy calling orders to the ship's hands or inspecting the equipment or talking to other passengers, inquiring about their comfort and welfare. Since the *Windsong* was used primarily to transport cargo rather than people, there were only a dozen or so passengers, and all of them seemed congenial and friendly. The journey that Margaret had expected to be long and tiresome was actually quite pleasant, and the time passed quickly.

On the eleventh morning after leaving Savannah, she had just finished her breakfast and walked out on the deck for a bit of fresh air when she heard a stir of voices. All of the passengers, it seemed, were gathered on the deck, straining their eyes and pointing.

"What is it?" she asked, peering in the direction of their apparent interest. Her eyes scanned the waves for a whale or some other unusual sea creature that might have captured their attention.

"Over there," an elderly gentleman told her. "See? You can see land over there. We must be coming into Tampa!"

Now Margaret could see the dark purple line that stretched across the horizon and knew that what the man said must be true. They were approaching their destination at last, and before the sun had set again, she would be in the arms of her beloved!

Shortly after noon, the *Windsong* sailed into Tampa Bay and crabbed its way into the port of Tampa, using only the drifter sail to ease its hull up close to the docks. Passengers lined the rails of the ship, while the hands struggled with the rigging, shouting phrases that Margaret did not understand.

"Loosen the lanyard; we're comin' about."

"Strike the drifter and ready the ratlines. Store the shrouds in the bin."

And finally, "She's ready; lower the plank."

With a great creak, a heavy, wooden ramp descended from the ship's side to the dock, and passengers hurried to disembark.

For the first time since she had left Savannah, Margaret began to feel a small nudge of apprehension. What was it like, this mysterious new land that would now be her home? And even more important, what was he like, the man with whom she had pledged to spend the rest of her life?

Margaret moved with the crowd along the sloping gangplank. Her heart raced with anticipation as she scanned the people waiting along the boardwalk bordering Tampa Bay. How would she ever find Allen Fairchild in all this mass of human flesh? People were shoving and pushing, shouting greetings when they spied familiar faces. She listened, but no one called her name.

What would she do if Allen did not come to meet her? She had not even considered that possibility. Now a lump formed in her throat and seemed to grow to the size of an egg.

She stood on the boardwalk and watched deckhands unload a portion of the cargo. Soon the *Windsong* would probably pull up anchor and continue on through the Gulf of Mexico toward New Orleans. She hoped they would not forget to unload her trunk!

All around her people were laughing and embracing, but there was not one familiar face among them. Panic began to engulf her as she scanned the crowds for a tall, handsome man in an army captain's uniform.

"Is someone coming to meet you, Margaret?"

Astonished to hear her name, she whipped around and looked up to see Mikal Lee towering over her, and for reasons she could not explain even to herself, her panic melted like butter on a hot griddle.

"Yes—well, that is, I hope so. You see. . ." But she gave up trying to talk to him over the noise of the crowd. Her green eyes were brimming with tears, which she struggled to contain.

Mikal gripped her elbow and steered her forward. "Let's

claim your luggage and go somewhere to talk."

Margaret moved like a child with no plan of her own. Perhaps Mikal would know how to help her find Allen. She let him guide her through the crowds.

"Which of these trunks is yours?" he asked, pointing to the piles of recently unloaded cargo. "Do you see it?"

"Yes." She pointed to a large, leather trunk with brass fittings. "That's mine. I have only the one."

Mikal released his grip on her elbow. "Don't move from this spot," he commanded.

As he disappeared into the mob, all of her earlier panic returned. "Don't leave me," she pleaded, but her voice was lost in the deafening cacophony of the crowd. She could no longer restrain the tears that now ran freely down her cheeks. Perhaps her father had been right after all, but it was too late to think of that now. Whatever was she to do?

Minutes later, Mikal reappeared at her side. "I've hired a carriage," he told her. "The driver is seeing to your trunk. Come on. We'll find a respectable boardinghouse where you can stay the night, and perhaps by morning, you will have heard from whomever was supposed to meet you."

"But how will he know where to find me?"

"The *Windsong* is staying in the port of Tampa for a couple of nights. If anyone comes here looking for you, I'll see that he is given proper directions."

She allowed him to lead her to the street and help her into a waiting carriage. She was surprised and relieved when he stepped up to claim the seat beside her. "Take us to Miss Priscilla's Boardinghouse," he commanded, and the carriage moved forward through the narrow dirt streets.

Margaret craned her neck for a better view of her new town. In her mind's eye, she had pictured a city similar to Savannah, with wide streets and stately homes fronted by columned porticos, but her conception was not even close.

The few stores they passed were constructed of dingy, unpainted boards, not at all like the beautiful brick commercial structures of Savannah. And the people themselves looked like plain, country folk. Most of the women she saw wore simple cotton dresses and covered their heads with calico bonnets, a far cry from the elegant matrons who shopped in Marshall's Emporium.

"Now that we can hear ourselves talk," Mikal said, "suppose you tell me the name of the person who was supposed to meet you and what you are planning to do in this part of the world."

Margaret held nothing back; she told him everything, from her contrived introduction to Allen Fairchild to her father's objections to the marriage, and finally of her disappointment at not being met at the pier.

Mikal took out a clean linen handkerchief and gave it to her. "Dry your tears, Margaret, and listen to me. There's probably a logical explanation for this. If your fiancé is in the army, he may be on duty tonight. A soldier's time is not his own, you know. He may be just as worried about missing your meeting as you are. Or it's possible that he may have never received your letter. The mail down here is very undependable. Do you have money?"

"A little. Not a lot, but enough to get along for a while."

"Then I suggest you get a room at Miss Priscilla's Boardinghouse, take a nice, hot bath, and sleep until morning. Priscilla will give you a good, hearty breakfast, and the world will look a lot better to you tomorrow. That's a promise."

"You are very kind to help me. Are you staying in Tampa long?"

"For only two days while the ship refuels and takes on extra passengers. I'm on my way to a port in the northwestern end of the territory called Apalachicola. I'll be sleeping in my stateroom on the schooner tonight, but I'll come in to check on you tomorrow. If you haven't heard from your friend by then, I'll take you to Fort Brooke and we'll try to find him. Meanwhile, try not to worry. Put yourself in God's hands, and He will take care of you."

The carriage stopped in front of a two-story, white frame house. Flowers bordered the walkway that split the grassy lawn. Cane rocking chairs on the porch gave the place an inviting look. A sign over the door read *Miss Priscilla's Boardinghouse*. And just beneath that was another sign: *Vacancy*.

"You'll be safe here," Mikal said, alighting from the carriage and swinging Margaret down beside him. "I'll help you make the arrangements before we unload your trunk."

Inside, Margaret met Miss Priscilla, a charming lady who ran an immaculate establishment. Mikal waited in the parlor while the two ladies went up the staircase to inspect the room.

Miss Priscilla paused at the head of the staircase and used a key to unlock the first door on her left. She held it wide and waited for Margaret to enter ahead of her. "This is it."

Margaret's eyes took in everything at a glance. The furniture, though not elegant, appeared comfortable and substantial. Crisp organdy curtains fluttered at the one open window facing the street. An oak washstand stood beside the iron bed frame and held a large china basin and pitcher. An oak chest of drawers and a small rocking chair were the only other furnishings. Several oval rag rugs graced the otherwise bare, whitewashed floor. Two large candlesticks rested on round lace doilies atop the dresser.

"There's a tub at the end of the hall. If you'll be wanting a bath, I'll have it filled for you, but that will be fifty cents extra."

"Oh, yes! I do want a bath."

"If you decide to take the room," Miss Priscilla continued, "I serve a hot breakfast in the dining room each morning at seven o'clock. If you should oversleep and miss breakfast, you will find fruit juice and crackers on the sideboard, but I do not cook but once."

"I understand. And I'll take the room," Margaret said without hesitation.

"One more thing," her landlady stated firmly. "No male visitors will be allowed in your room. Your friend is not to go beyond the parlor."

Margaret flushed. "Of course not." *What kind of lady does she think I am?* Margaret wondered. She held up her skirts and followed her landlady back down the stairs.

Mikal watched Margaret descend the wooden staircase. She was a beautiful woman, and his heart went out to her in all her troubles. He prayed that he could find some way to help her. "Well, Margaret, what do you think?"

"I'm staying," she told him, "and I don't know how to thank you for all your help."

"No thanks are necessary. I assure you, it is my pleasure. I'll have your trunk taken up to your room, and then I'll be on my way, but just remember what I've told you, Margaret. Turn all your troubles over to God, and try not to worry. I'll be back to check on you before noon tomorrow."

Mikal helped the driver carry the heavy trunk up the stairs, and the two men placed it at the foot of the bed, while Margaret stood in the hallway giving them directions.

At last everything was settled, and Mikal climbed back into the horse-drawn carriage.

Margaret stood on the porch and waved until the carriage was out of sight. Mikal Lee had spread a temporary cloak of security around her, and even though a thousand unanswered questions whirled through her mind, she knew that she had found a dependable friend to lean on.

She returned to the room that was now her home, without even the slightest premonition of the precarious situation in which her headstrong actions had placed her.

two

Unfamiliar sounds dragged Margaret from a puzzling dream. She had been standing on a swaying deck surrounded by rolling whitecaps as far as the eye could see. As the schooner skimmed through the waves toward shore, she could see Allen Fairchild on the dock with both hands in the air, waving to her. But what she could not understand was why his hair was no longer black—the dark strands had mysteriously changed to blond, the color of fine corn silk, curling softly where it met the edge of his collar.

As she struggled into awareness, she realized that she wasn't swaying at all, and the noises she heard were more akin to street sounds than ocean waves.

Morning sun filtered through the white organdy curtains and slanted across the bedroom. Margaret sat up and rubbed her eyes. It took her several minutes to reconstruct the events that had led her to this unfamiliar place, but now she remembered it all: Mikal Lee had brought her here to Miss Priscilla's Boardinghouse, and he had promised to return today to help her find Allen Fairchild.

The clatter of dishes and the aroma of coffee floated up from downstairs, reminding her that she had not eaten since yesterday noon. Now her stomach rumbled to protest its emptiness.

She had been too tired and distraught to even think of food last night; she barely remembered having her bath and tumbling into bed. As she had sunk her head into the goose-down pillow, Mikal's words about turning over her problems to God had echoed in her mind. It was a fact that she surely needed someone to turn them over to, but she doubted that God would listen to her. She had not tried to communicate with Him in a very long time. Still, it wouldn't hurt to try.

Her last waking thoughts were of trying to recall the prayers her mother had taught her before her sudden and untimely death. But Margaret had been only six years old when her mother died, and now she could not get beyond "Now I lay me down to sleep."

At that point, sleep had claimed her mind and body and plunged her into a night of senseless dreams. Now in the light of morning, she still felt tired. Mikal had promised that things would seem better today. Perhaps they would after she placated her growling stomach with a hearty breakfast.

The bare floor felt cold against her feet. She stood on a rag rug to open her trunk and choose her clothes for the day.

Wistfully, she eyed her trousseau dresses, all carefully folded and packed in happy anticipation of her life in a new world with Allen Fairchild. She had spent many long hours standing patiently before her Savannah dressmaker while the skilled seamstress measured and pinned, unsatisfied with anything less than a perfect fit.

Passing through the streets of Tampa yesterday, Margaret had been surprised at the plain way the local women seemed to dress. Margaret had never owned anything that even remotely resembled their homespun attire. She selected the most simple gown in her trunk: a yellow faille dress with a high, unadorned neckline, and decided that she would wear only one crinoline beneath her skirts today.

She lifted her new, lace-trimmed chemise and pantalettes from the tissue in which she had wrapped them and began to dress for breakfast. She hoped that Miss Priscilla would have a nice, fresh omelet and a bowl of hot grits! Hot tea would be nice, too. My, she was hungry!

Her skirts rustled as she descended the stairs, causing the olive-skinned maid to pause from her chores and look up.

"Oh, mornin', miss!"

"Good morning," Margaret replied politely. "Where should I sit for breakfast?"

"Oh, miss, I'm very sorry. Breakfast was served at seven, and it's now half after eight. But there's some fresh-squeezed orange juice on the sideboard. I picked the oranges and squeezed them myself this morning," she ended proudly.

"But. . .but. . .why wasn't I called? Where is Miss Priscilla? I must speak to her at once!"

"Miss Priscilla, she left to go to market 'bout ten minutes ago, but she'll be back directly. Oh, missy, I'm real sorry you didn't know 'bout the time. You pour yourself some juice and sit down here at the table, and I'll go out to the kitchen and see if I can get you a biscuit, but you mustn't tell Miss Priscilla!"

With a wink of her dark eyes, the petite maid disappeared, and Margaret sat alone at the long, wooden table. Her thoughts drifted to Savannah, where her father was probably this very minute sitting at his own dining table, enjoying his third cup of coffee while he read the morning newspaper. She could almost smell the bacon and eggs!

Margaret was munching on a cold, dry biscuit, washing it down with a tall glass of orange juice, when Mikal arrived.

"I hope I haven't kept you waiting," he said as he drew up a chair beside her. "I had to see to some things on the *Windsong* before I could leave."

"No, I just got up. I'm afraid I overslept breakfast," she admitted with a sheepish smile.

"Well, don't worry about that. There's a clean café between here and Fort Brooke. We can stop for food along the way."

"No, this will be enough to sustain me. I'm anxious to get on to Fort Brooke to find Allen. Is it far from here?"

"Oh, no. We're practically there now. You see, in 1824, when our government moved the Seminole Indians to a reservation near here, they built Fort Brooke and sent in army troops to oversee it. A few years back, Tampa was just a simple fishing village, but now that Fort Brooke has grown up around it, things are beginning to look more prosperous."

"Indians? Are there *Indians* around here?" Margaret darted her eyes around the room as though she half-expected to see a red-skinned warrior lurking in one of the corners.

"Well, of course there are. Lots of them. But these days, you aren't likely to see any of them walking down the street. Under orders from President Andrew Jackson, the government is forcing all the Seminole Indians to relocate to Oklahoma, and many of them simply refuse to go. They're willing to risk their lives to stay in their native homeland, and many have gone into hiding in the woods. That's what this conflict between the army and the Seminoles is all about."

"Yes, Allen explained that to me, but I didn't realize—" Margaret lowered her voice to a whisper. "Is the maid here an Indian?"

Mikal laughed. "No, she's a Spanish señorita—or maybe she's a señora. In any case, you'll see lots of Spanish people around these parts. Remember, this territory belonged to Spain until 1821. If you live here for very long, you'll probably learn to speak their language."

When pigs fly! Margaret finished her juice and biscuit without comment and wiped her lips on her napkin.

"Are you ready, then? I have a carriage waiting outside."

"Just let me run upstairs and get my bonnet and reticule. I'll be right back down."

Margaret returned to her room and lifted a yellow baize bonnet from her trunk. She adjusted it over her hair and tied it beneath her chin by its satin ribbons. She picked up her black velvet reticule from the dresser and hurried downstairs, locking her bedroom door behind her.

As she started down the stairs, she experienced a strange mixture of anticipation and apprehension. *What will I really feel when I come face to face with Allen Fairchild again?*

Mikal held the front door open for her and led her down the walk. He helped her into the waiting hackney and gave directions to the driver before he climbed up and took his seat beside her.

As the carriage moved along the narrow, dirt street, Margaret was interested in everything around her. Was this strange place now to be her home? Women with baskets over their arms walked the streets with small children clinging to their calico skirts. Most wore beehive bonnets to shade their faces from the bright morning sun. The carriage blew up a flurry of dust in its wake, and street vendors ran along beside it shouting their wares.

A child no more than six, a thin, ragamuffin little girl, raced alongside the hackney, shouting to be heard above the noise of the wheels. "Flowers, mister? Flowers for the lady?" She clutched a pitiful bouquet of wildflowers in her hand. In her effort to keep up with the carriage, she stumbled on the stones in the road and sprawled headlong into the dirt, scattering her flowers on the street.

"Stop!" Mikal called to the driver. When the carriage wheels slowed to a standstill, he climbed down and lifted the little girl to her feet. He used his handkerchief to brush the dust from her skinned knees and her tattered skirt. "Are you all right?"

Wide, frightened eyes met his, and the child only nodded. As she groped for her fallen flowers, Mikal took them from her and placed some coins in her hand. "I need these for the lady," he explained.

The little girl rewarded him with a wide, snaggle-toothed grin before she ran happily down the street, clutching the money in her tiny hand, calling, "Mama! Mama, look! The man buyed all my flowers! See what he gived me?"

Smiling, Mikal swung himself back into the carriage and

waited until they were well along the way before he tossed the wilted bouquet out onto the ground.

"Is that child someone you know?" Margaret asked.

"No, I've never seen her before. But this is a very poor area. Many of the settlers who've come down here believing this to be a land of opportunity are having a hard time just getting by."

The houses they passed were little more than shanties. Margaret could not imagine setting up housekeeping in one of them. The few stores sprinkled along the road were simple, whitewashed structures, and Margaret saw nothing that evenly remotely compared to Marshall's Emporium in Savannah.

An open-air market was crowded with men, women, and children bartering for produce and other merchandise.

Although theirs was the only carriage on the road, men on horseback traveled in both directions, causing street dust to rise like a great, persistent cloud. Margaret pulled a lace-edged handkerchief from her reticule and covered her nose, but the dust seemed to penetrate the cloth, causing her to cough. "Are those men on horses real cowboys?" she asked.

"Cow*hunters*," Mikal corrected. "That's what they're called in the territory. They build up their herds by gathering wild cattle and claim ownership by branding them."

"They all seem to carry guns. Are they outlaws?"

"I suppose some of them might be, but most are just honest, hard-working men trying to make a living for their families. The guns are for protection, but not just from outlaws. They have to worry about rattlesnakes and wolves and. . ." Suddenly seeming to sense Margaret's growing alarm, he hastened to add, "The cowhunters have to go way out through the woods and in the swamps in places you won't ever be likely to go. They have to be prepared for most anything."

The road became even bumpier as they moved along. *Like a washboard,* Margaret thought.

At last, the road ended at a wide, wooden façade that stretched across the road. A sign spanned the top, with letters burned into the wood proclaiming this to be Fort Brooke.

Mikal stepped down from the carriage and talked to the guard at the gate. Margaret could not hear their words, but she could see that they were involved in a heated discussion. After several minutes, the soldier opened the gates and let them pass through.

"That wooden building over there is the office of the base commander," Mikal called to his driver. As they drew up to the colorless structure, Margaret noted that the stark landscape was relieved by neither trees nor shrubbery. A hitching post by the front door secured one lone horse.

"You wait in the carriage, and I'll go inside to see what I can find out," Mikal told her.

"No, I want to come with you. I want to find out where Allen is."

It would have been useless for Mikal to protest, because Margaret was already scrambling out of the carriage behind him.

The office was nothing more than one small room cluttered with books and papers. A rotund officer rose from behind the only desk and eyed them suspiciously. "I am Major Copperfield. What can I do for you?"

Before Mikal could explain the situation, Margaret pushed him aside. "I've come to see Captain Allen Fairchild. I know he is here somewhere! Where are you keeping him?" Her voice bordered on hysteria.

Major Copperfield looked at her in disbelief. "Madam, who sent you here? We do not allow visitors inside the fort without a special pass. May I see yours?"

Mikal gently gripped Margaret's arm and pulled her back from the desk. "Please, Margaret. Just sit down for a moment and let me talk to the major."

The hours of stress, coupled with hunger, finally caught up with Margaret, and she collapsed onto the nearest chair and let Mikal take over to state her concerns to the commanding officer.

"Major Copperfield," Mikal began, "Miss Porter has come all the way from Savannah to meet her fiancé, Allen Fairchild. They are to be married, but when he was not at the dock to meet her last evening, she became concerned, and she has not yet heard from him since she arrived at the port of Tampa. Your sentry was kind enough to let us pass to see if you could help us locate the gentleman in question."

Mikal's calm manner seemed to placate the major, and he said, "I'll see what I can do." He stepped across the room and pulled out a box from the corner. Watching him riffle through the papers in the box, Mikal wondered how he could ever decipher its contents, but after several minutes the officer pulled a folder from the box. "Yes, here it is."

Margaret rose and watched his expression as he turned the sheets in the folder. She held her breath and waited for him to tell her what she had come here to learn. *Where is Allen Fairchild?*

Major Copperfield did not speak at once. His face turned a purplish-red, and beads of perspiration stood out on his brow. He pulled a handkerchief from his pocket and wiped his forehead. He turned the pages over in his hands and looked at them again and again, as though expecting the written words to change. The silence in the room lay as thick as a winter fog until he broke it at last by saying, "Madam, I think you should sit down to hear this."

He could not meet her eyes as he told her the dreaded news. Captain Allen Fairchild had returned from his leave in December only ten days before his company, under the direction of Major Francis Dade, met with a terrible misfortune. They were on their way north to Fort King on the coldest night in

December. Halfway there, they were ambushed by a group of savage Indians, and when the bloody massacre ended, only three men lived to tell about it. The major finished by saying that two of the three survivors had since died from their wounds.

Margaret stood beside the chair and listened in wide-eyed horror, but as Mikal moved toward her, she pitched forward and lay limp and lifeless on the bare wooden floor.

"Margaret!" Mikal scooped her up in his arms. "Do you have first aid supplies? A cloth and some cold water or some smelling salts, perhaps?"

"No, I keep nothing here. I say, this is highly irregular. . ."

"Where is your infirmary? We must take her there."

"Follow me."

Mikal lifted Margaret's limp body into the waiting carriage while Major Copperfield untied his horse from the hitching post.

As the wagon driver followed the officer on horseback, Mikal cradled her in his arms and tried to absorb the bumps. Just as they drew up before a long, wooden barracks building, Margaret's eyelids began to flutter. "Mikal?"

"I'm here, Margaret. We're going to take good care of you." He helped her to a sitting position, supporting her with his arm. "This is the infirmary. You've had a great shock, and you need medical attention."

Her forehead wrinkled as she tried to dredge up memories that would explain why she was here, but as the major's horrible words crept back into her consciousness, she screamed, "No!" Then with a tremor in her voice, she begged, "Please, Mikal. Just take me home. They have no medicine here that can cure my grief. I want to get away from this dreadful place. I just want to go home and be alone."

"As you wish, then. Just give me a moment to speak to the major."

Mikal knew that Margaret would have questions later after she recovered from her initial shock. He wanted to have some answers ready for her.

He approached Major Copperfield and listened as the officer related all the facts as he knew them. Allen Fairchild's body lay buried in an unmarked grave somewhere along the trail to Fort King.

"Is there anything of the captain's that you might give to the lady? Some small token of his that she might keep?" Mikal asked.

"Captain Fairchild's few personal effects were sent to his parents, but it is doubtful they will ever receive them. The territory is a lawless land, Mr. Lee, and unfortunately only a very small percentage of our mail ever reaches its destination. I'm sorry," Major Copperfield said. "I wish there was something I could do to help."

"I'm afraid there's nothing either of us can do."

Mikal returned to the carriage and gave orders to the driver to turn around. Then, taking his place beside Margaret, he waved his thanks to Major Copperfield and the horse-driven carriage began to retrace its earlier route.

Mikal held Margaret's trembling body in his arms and let her cry. No longer interested in the dramas being played out around her, she buried her head in Mikal's shoulder and allowed unrestrained tears to flow. They rode through the village of Tampa in a shroud of silence, interrupted only by the sound of hoofbeats and the soft sobs of Margaret Porter.

three

Margaret sat on the sofa in Miss Priscilla's parlor, her eyes clouded with confusion. Pain was overshadowed by the numbness that permeated her whole being. The events of the morning seemed like a dream from which she must soon awake and cast aside, just as she had cast aside her strange dream of the night before.

Mikal sat across from her in a Sheraton chair, his long legs crossed at the knees. Earlier, he had spoken to Miss Priscilla and explained the unfortunate situation. In a rare burst of sympathy, the landlady had provided a tea tray in the parlor, breaking one of her own steadfast rules about taking food into her keeping room.

"Is there anyone in the territory whom I could contact to come be with you, Margaret?" It tore at Mikal's heart to see her sitting there alone, so fragile and defenseless, sipping her tea from a thin porcelain cup. He yearned to comfort her.

Her hand shook so that when she set her teacup down, it rattled against the saucer. "No, I don't know anyone here except you, Mikal. I know I've been a terrible burden for you, and I'm sorry. You don't need to stay here with me any longer. As soon as I can pull myself together, I'll figure out what I'm going to do next."

"Margaret, I truly don't want to leave you, but I have to be on the *Windsong* when she sails tomorrow morning. I wish that I had a choice in the matter, but I don't. We'll make our regular run up to Apalachicola to unload our cargo of textiles, and then we'll reload the ship with cotton brought down the Apalachicola River from Georgia and Alabama. Then we'll turn the ship around and head back to New York." Seeing her eyes wander about the room, he said, "Margaret, are you listening to me?"

"Yes, I'm listening, but I have a lot of things on my mind, Mikal, and I don't see what any of this has to do with me."

"I'm coming to that. Don't you see? When we return from Apalachicola, we'll be stopping over in the port of Tampa again. I'll have to be gone for the next several weeks, but as soon as I return, you can rebook passage on the *Windsong*, and I will take you back home to your father in Savannah."

Margaret hung her head and did not answer for several minutes. Mikal had been so kind to her, and she knew that he only wanted to help her. But how could she explain to him the complicated reasons why she could not return to Savannah?

First, there was the matter of her father. He had been so terribly angry with her for leaving. How would he feel now about having her return? And what a lot of pride she would have to swallow! His dire predictions about the foolishness of her plans were proving to be all too true.

And then there was the matter of money. There was simply not enough money in her black velvet reticule to pay for return passage to Savannah. If she could find some sort of employment, perhaps in time she could save enough for her fare, but certainly not within the next few weeks. And what possible talent could she offer to any potential employer? She had never earned even a half-dime in her whole life.

She could not tell Mikal of her financial problems without sounding as though she were hinting for his charity. Of course, no respectable lady would accept money from a gentleman, even if he should happen to offer it. In fact, she would consider such an offer a personal insult.

Mikal interpreted her long silence to mean that she was in agreement with his plan. "I'll speak to Miss Priscilla to make sure you'll be allowed to have room and board here until I return. You'll be safe here and moderately comfortable. I've been praying for guidance about this, Margaret, and I know that everything is going to work out for the best. We just have to put our faith in God."

Margaret jerked to attention. "How can you talk to me about God at a time like this?" she yelled. "What kind of God would let a bunch of savages murder a nice man like Allen Fairchild? Answer me that before you talk to me about having faith in your God!"

Mikal, remaining in his chair, planted both feet on the floor and clasped his hands between his knees. He let her rant and rave until her energy was spent. She had suffered a severe shock today. Perhaps she needed to vent her anger. Sometimes the steam in the boilers of a steamship built up to a dangerous level and had to be released to avoid a devastating explosion. Release could be a good thing, up to a point.

When Margaret finished her tirade, she sank back against the cushions and let her tears escape. She wondered that her eyes had not run dry of tears by now, but still they came in cold rivulets, running down her fiery cheeks.

"I'm sorry I've upset you, Margaret. Perhaps you'd rather be alone for a while. In any case, I have to return to the schooner and be ready to sail at dawn." He rose. "I really hate to leave you this way, but I have no choice." He grasped her hands and pulled her to her feet. "Walk with me out to the porch. I want to look back and see you waving to me. I'll carry that memory all the way to Apalachicola and back, and then we'll talk again about your plans for the future. Please trust me, Margaret, and. . ."

Anticipating his next words, she cut him off by saying, "Thank you for all your help, Mikal. I'm sorry if I was rude. I didn't mean to be. It's just that I'm not myself today. By the time you return, I'll have myself pulled together and be able to tell you what I've decided to do."

He did not call for a carriage, preferring a brisk walk in the cool night air. The setting sun had cast a soft, pink-tinged glow across the horizon, and the streets seemed quieter and cleaner in the twilight.

She watched him walk down the street until he blended into the crowds, and when she could no longer identify him, she turned back into the house and went upstairs to her room.

๛

Miss Priscilla served supper promptly at six o'clock. "We eat a little later in the summer when the days are longer," she explained, "but in the winter, we try to conserve our candles by eating early."

Margaret sat at the long, rectangular table and helped herself from the platters of food as they passed her way. Fried chicken, sweet potatoes, and collard greens made the rounds, and although Margaret had little appetite, she put a small portion of each dish on her plate. She told herself that she must build up her strength for the trying days ahead. She could not go around fainting as she had this morning, especially now that Mikal would no longer be around to pick her up.

One by one, the other boarders introduced themselves, and Margaret acknowledged them each with a nod. The two gentlemen, Patrick Anderson and Charles Jeffries, were dressed in a manner that suggested to Margaret that they both might be barristers. The elderly Rosada sisters, Hope and Charity, shared a room next to Margaret's. Their demure, black and white print dresses were almost identical, as were the twists of white hair each wore coiled atop her head. A young woman, whom Margaret judged to be only slightly older than herself, was introduced as Mrs. Lucy White, a young widow. She was modestly dressed in black cotton, fashioned in the austere style that seemed to prevail in this area, and her sandy brown hair was caught in a loose bun at the nape of her neck.

Miss Priscilla sat tall and erect, presiding at the head of the table with a small crystal bell beside her plate, which she used from time to time to summon help from the kitchen.

Margaret listened with only a modicum of interest to the chatter around her. "I hear there's a rumor going around that the Florida Territory might be coming into the Union before long," one of the Rosada sisters said. "Would there be any truth to that, Mr. Jeffries?"

"Not if that bunch up in St. Augustine has their way!"

"But the people up in the western part of the territory have something to say about that, too," Patrick Anderson pointed out. "They're making plans for a Constitution Convention, I hear. Wonder who the delegates will be?"

"I wouldn't mind being a part of that," Charles Jeffries admitted. "And if I couldn't be a delegate, I'd sure like to be a mouse so I could listen in."

"I was a delegate once," Miss Charity stated proudly, "to the Ladies' Missionary Society in Virginia. I believe that was back in 1779."

"It wasn't '79; it was 1778. And you weren't a delegate at all, Sister. You were just attending as a member from our local church," Miss Hope insisted.

"Delegate, member, what's the difference, Sister? At least I got to attend." A satisfied smile spread across Miss Charity's face. "As I recall, you were a little miffed that Papa wouldn't let you go."

"Only because I was so much *younger*," Miss Hope retorted, determined to have the last and best word.

Margaret wanted to excuse herself to escape from this conversation, which did not interest her in the least, but she did not want to appear rude. She sat quietly and listened until Miss Priscilla rang for the maid and dessert was served.

"Indian pudding!" Miss Charity exclaimed. "My favorite."

"Now, Sister, just last night you said that sweet potato pie was your favorite!"

"Well, it *was* my favorite last night, Sister. But tonight my favorite is Indian pudding!"

The two gentlemen exchanged amused glances, while Lucy hid her smile behind her white linen napkin.

"Miss Priscilla, would you excuse me, please?" Margaret asked. "I–I'm unable—that is, I've had a very trying day, so if you will all excuse me, I think I will retire to my room."

"Of course, Margaret. We understand."

Soft murmurs of consent circled the table, confirming Margaret's belief that Miss Priscilla had already told her other boarders of the tragedy that had struck her life today.

She pushed her chair away from the table, rose, and saw the two gentlemen rise in unison. "No, please, gentlemen. Keep your seats."

She turned from the table and hurried up the stairs.

In the privacy of her room, Margaret pulled down the window shades and changed into her chemise. She poured water from her pitcher into her washbowl and used her hands to splash some of it on her face before drying on the clean linen towel.

She emptied the money from her reticule onto the bed and counted it. She tried to calculate the amount she would need for room and board for the weeks ahead. Mikal had told her he would not be back for several weeks, and even then she would not have money for passage back to Savannah. Whether she returned or not, she would need money just to live on. She would simply have to find a source of income.

She looked in her trunk and tried to decide what she owned of value that she might try to sell. The only jewelry she had brought with her was a single strand of pearls and her mother's cameo brooch. Nothing could make her part with that brooch. She would starve first! But perhaps she could find someone who would buy her pearls. Her father had given them to her on her sixteenth birthday. They were real pearls and should fetch a good price.

In the fading light of dusk, she replaced her money into her reticule and put it in her top dresser drawer, along with the velvet pouch that held her beautiful pearls. Rather than light a candle, she pulled back the bedspread and stretched across the cool, cotton sheets.

Lying on her bed in the darkness, she listened to the unfamiliar night sounds. Dogs barking, horses trotting rhythmically along the dirt street, and the occasional creak of wagon wheels. *How can they see to travel in the dark?* she wondered. Somewhere a baby cried, and from the direction of Tampa Bay, she heard the distant whistle of a steamboat.

She thought of Mikal and the *Windsong* and knew that by the time she woke up in the morning, they would both be gone. Would Mikal really return for her as he had promised, or would he forget all about her once he was out on the vast Gulf of Mexico? And if he did return to take her back to Savannah, would she find some honorable way to go with him? These and a dozen other questions spun in her head like a tornado.

Mikal had told her to put herself in God's hands, but she was mad at God right now, and He was evidently mad at her, too. If He cared for her the way Mikal had told her, He would never have let her end up in such a terrible predicament.

But here alone in her room, she had no one else to whom she could turn. Out of desperation, she slid from her bed and knelt on the cold, wooden floor. "God, if You can hear me and You really care what happens to me, show me some way out of this corner I've backed myself into. Amen."

She climbed back into bed and stared through the darkness at the ceiling. If she had some way to make sure that her father would welcome her back to live with him in Savannah and if she had some way to get enough money for her passage, then returning home would be the logical solution to her problems.

She would write him a letter tomorrow, admitting her mistakes and asking his forgiveness. She would ask him to send money for her passage home. Father had never refused to give her anything she had asked him for. Surely he would not let her down now.

But the mails were slow and uncertain, especially where money was involved. She had heard lurid tales of outlaws down here in the wilds of the Florida Territory who made a habit of robbing the mail carriers along the postal routes. Even if her father received her letter and sent the money, would it ever reach her?

Then a new idea popped into her mind, and she thought that perhaps God really was on her side after all! She would write the letter to her father and ask Mikal to deliver it to him in Savannah, asking him to wait for an answer. If her father still loved her and wanted her back, he would give Mikal enough money to bring her back home.

If her new plan worked out, then all her worries might soon be over. But there were an awful lot of "ifs" to conquer before her plan could have even the slightest chance of success.

four

Margaret kept to her room for a full week, coming out only for meals served in the dining room.

The first job that she tackled was the writing of the all-important letter to her father. She had wasted a dozen sheets of her prettiest stationery, writing and rewriting the letter, before she finally came up with what she hoped would be the right words to touch his heart and win his forgiveness. The sum of money she requested was only slightly more than the amount she would need to pay for passage on the *Windsong*, but if her father came through in his usual style, Margaret was sure that he would include a generous lagniappe.

She had little doubt that he would honor her request, and now she had only to figure a way to stretch her limited resources so that they would last until her money arrived.

Once she was satisfied with the letter, she folded it into thirds and dripped a dot of sealing wax on the back to secure it. She put it in her top drawer for safekeeping and tried to put it out of her mind until Mikal returned.

She passed away some of her long, lonely hours by flipping through the pages of Miss Priscilla's newest issue of *Ladies' Book*, which featured all of Godey's latest fashions. She supposed that even women who dressed as conservatively as Miss Priscilla still enjoyed seeing what fashionable ladies in the States were wearing. Margaret derived satisfaction from knowing that the clothes in her trunk bore a striking resemblance to the ones featured in this latest issue of *Ladies' Book*. Not that she would have occasion to wear them here in the wilds of the Florida Territory, but some day she vowed she would wear them and feel like a real lady again.

But regardless of how inappropriate her elegant dresses might be, they were all that she had, and she couldn't stay here in her room forever. There was no reason for her to procrastinate any longer about going into the village of Tampa and looking for a buyer for her pearls.

She wondered if people here would expect her to observe a period of mourning. In truth, although she did feel very sad about the tragic death of her fiancé, and especially in knowing the agony he must have suffered at the hands of the Seminoles, she realized now that her love for Allen Fairchild had been based on a young girl's fantasy. Perhaps she would have grown to love him in time, but having been deprived of that chance, she must now put the past behind her and look to the future.

She was not the same naïve young girl who less than a month ago had left her Savannah home seeking romance and adventure. Her experiences of these past weeks had begun to give her a maturity and insight that she would never have attained in the protective custody of her father. She had a new life now, with new responsibilities, and she must go out and face them on her own.

For her trip to the village, she chose a forest green gown of softest piqué, fashioned along princess lines. Her dressmaker had made a stunning bonnet of the same material, lined with a softer shade of green that she was told brought out the color of her eyes. Her face was circled with a narrow band of pleated ruffling that outlined the bonnet's brim, with a small cluster of purple violets nestled over one ear.

Margaret adjusted the bonnet over her hair and tied its satin ribbons beneath her chin. Smoothing her skirts, she set out for her first visit alone into the little village of Tampa, her single strand of pearls tucked securely in her reticule.

Walking along the street toward the market, she lifted her

skirts just a little to avoid the dust that swirled around her ankles. She was aware of the curious stares of the people she passed, both men and women, but she walked along at a brisk gait with her head held high.

The sun beat down on her shoulders, causing her to wish that she had brought along her parasol. In Savannah, she would not have expected such heat at this time of the year.

She did not pause at the open-air market, but continued instead to a long, rectangular building with a tin roof and an open front porch. The sign over the door said *Bowden's General Store.*

Margaret gathered her courage and entered through the double screen door. The buzz of shoppers was abruptly silenced the moment she stepped inside, and she felt all the eyes turn in her direction.

"Kin I he'p you, miss?" A white-haired gentlemen clad in overalls approached her cautiously, letting his eyes travel over her elegant green gown.

"Why, yes. I would like to speak to the proprietor, please."

"That'd be me, ma'am. What kin I do fer ya?"

A curious circle of people gathered close to hear what the lady had to say.

"Is there some place where I could speak to you privately?" Margaret asked. She had no desire to share her problems with all the customers in the store.

The old man looked puzzled for a few moments. Then his face brightened. "I reckon we could step out on the porch."

Margaret supposed that this was the best that she could hope for, so she followed him out the door. "Sir," she began, "I am new to this area. Is there a merchant here who deals in fine jewelry?"

"Well, no ma'am, not exactly, but I do have a few nice pieces I keep in my lockbox. What was you alookin' fer?"

"No, you don't understand." Margaret lowered her voice to

a whisper. "I don't want to buy anything. I have something I want to sell." She pulled the pearls from her reticule and spread them across her palm. "These are genuine, natural pearls. I–I find it necessary to dispose of them. Do you know who might help me find a buyer for them?"

The merchant scratched his white head and squinted his eyes. "Well, there ain't nobody else but me, and I reckon I could try to sell 'em fer you. How much was you awantin' fer 'em?"

Margaret quoted a figure that was not even half of their value, but she was desperate to conclude a quick transaction. "I–I'd sacrifice them for two hundred dollars."

The old man's eyes bulged. "Ma'am, they ain't many people in Tampa with that kind of money. I do git some of the wives of the Fort Brooke officers in here lookin' fer somethin' extra special, but I don't know as they would go that high." Seeing Margaret's crestfallen face, he added, "If'n you want to leave 'em here, I'll see what I kin do. Check back with me in a week, an' if I've had any offers, I'll tell you. Then if'n you decide to sell, you can pay me ten percent. How does that sound to you?"

Margaret was reluctant to hand over her precious pearls to a complete stranger, but she did not know what else to do. "Would you write me out a receipt for them?"

"Yes'm. I kin do that."

She followed him back into the store where he found a pencil and a scrap of paper. "You write what you want on here, an' I'll sign it," he said.

Margaret wrote in her ornate penmanship: *Received from Margaret Porter, one perfect strand of natural pearls.* She dated the note and gave it to him to sign.

Much to her surprise, the man summoned his wife. "Ola May, come over here, honey. I need you to he'p me sign this paper." As the man carefully drew a large X on the paper, a plump woman in an apron-covered calico dress stepped up to sign as his witness.

She fingered the pearls her husband held in his hand. "My, ain't them pretty?" she said, smiling at her new customer. "You sure you want to let go of these?"

"No—I mean, yes. Of course. I'm sure," Margaret stammered, and turned to go. The doorway was blocked by two women who stood whispering together. Each of them wore pastel muslin gowns, causing them to stand out against the other customers, most of whom wore plain, homespun frocks faded beyond color recognition.

Margaret was sure by the focus of their eyes that they were talking about her. As she tried to move past them, the taller woman spoke to her. "Please excuse me for being so forward. I'm Katherine, and my friend Meli and I were just admiring your bonnet."

"Thank you," Margaret said. She returned their smiles, thinking that one of these ladies just might be the customer who would purchase her strand of pearls.

"You're new to the area, aren't you?" Meli asked. "We were remarking that we had not seen you in the store before."

Margaret introduced herself and explained that she had only been here for a little better than a week and that she was exploring the village today so that she would know where to shop.

"Shop?" Katherine said with a laugh. "You won't be able to do much shopping in Tampa. Every few weeks a boat comes in from the States, and new merchandise is purchased for the store here, but anything good goes out the door the same day it comes in. You really have to keep an eye out for the boats when they dock and be on hand to buy what you like before someone else does."

"I'll keep that in mind," Margaret promised, knowing full well that she would not be able to buy anything beyond the bare essentials. She tried once again to move past them, but Katherine laid a hand on her arm.

"Margaret, I don't want to be rude, but I simply must know where you purchased your bonnet. I have a new green dress, and I'd give anything to have one like it."

"You would?" Margaret's mind was already beginning to whirl. Her hand reached up to pull the ribbons and release her bonnet. She slid it off her hair and handed it to Katherine. "Would you like to examine it more closely? Really, I have more bonnets than I can possibly use down here. I don't know whatever possessed me to bring so many. If you really would like to have this one, I suppose I could part with it for—say, about five dollars?" Margaret held her breath. Five dollars was a lot of money. Had she gone too far?

But the words were barely out of her mouth when Katherine reached into her reticule and pulled out five silver Liberty dollars. It was apparent that she intended to seal the transaction before Margaret could change her mind.

Margaret slipped the coins into her own handbag, listening to the satisfying jingle they made when they dropped inside.

"Well, that's not fair," Meli pouted. "I'm the one who noticed your bonnet first. If I had known you would part with it, I'd have offered you six."

Six dollars! Almost enough to pay room and board at Miss Priscilla's for two more weeks! "Meli, I don't want to see you disappointed. Do you like blue? I have a lovely blue satin bonnet that would just match your eyes. I could bring it to you tomorrow, if you'd like."

Meli's eyes lit up like a child who'd just seen a Christmas tree. "Oh, yes, yes! I do love blue. What time shall I meet you here tomorrow?"

"Let's come early before the sun gets too high," Margaret suggested. "How about nine o'clock?"

"I'll be here," Meli exclaimed. "Are you sure the blue one is just as pretty as Katherine's?"

"It's even prettier," Margaret promised. "That's why it's worth an extra dollar." She did not want to give Meli a chance to forget that she had promised to pay her six dollars.

This time the ladies let her pass through the door. As Margaret walked down the porch steps, she could hear the silver coins jingling in her reticule. She was not sure whether Mr. Bowden would find a buyer for her pearls or not, but as long as her supply of bonnets held out, she could take care of herself until the money from her father arrived.

five

After supper one evening, as Margaret sat in the parlor leafing through a copy of *Ladies' Companion*, Lucy White came in and sat beside her on the sofa. Lucy was wearing a severely styled black dress, just as she always did, but she eyed the colorful pages wistfully. "I'll be glad when my period of mourning is over," she said. "It's been almost a year since I've worn anything other than black."

"But why do you have to always wear black?" Margaret asked. "Wouldn't a soft, pastel dress be just as appropriate?"

Lucy looked as shocked as if Margaret had suggested she appear in public in her underwear. "But it wouldn't be proper. Not for a year, anyway."

"I'm sorry. I didn't mean to sound disrespectful. I'm sure that losing your husband must have been very painful for you. Were you married for a very long time?"

"Only ten days," Lucy said. "I was just getting to know him. You see, I came to the territory from Massachusetts as a mail-order bride, but two days after Tom and I were married, he came down with pneumonia, and in just one week, he was dead."

"How very sad," Margaret sympathized. She had never met a mail-order bride before. "Will you be returning to Mass-achusetts soon?"

"Oh, no. As soon as my year of mourning is over, I aim to get married again."

Margaret did not know how she should reply to this. "That. . .that will be very nice for you. Who is the lucky man?"

"Well, I don't know yet," Lucy told her. "There's lots of men in the territory advertising for wives. Would you be interested in meeting one?"

Margaret felt the blood rush to her cheeks. "Oh, no! No thank you. Isn't it a little scary marrying a stranger?"

"Indeed it is! But good men are scarce up where I come from. At least, they are when you get to be my age."

Margaret thought that Lucy was not an unattractive woman, and she wondered why she had needed to come so far to find a husband. But she did not need to ask, because Lucy had already begun to explain.

"During the years when all my friends were getting married, I was nursing an invalid mother. My sisters both married and moved away, and there wasn't anyone else around to take care of Mama, so I stayed. By the time she died, I was already thirty years old, and most of the men I knew were already married. Those who were left were courting girls in their twenties. I felt that time was running out, so I answered an ad in a Boston newspaper and packed up my things and came down here to the Florida Territory. I don't think I'll marry a soldier next time, though. I've decided I want a man who stays home."

"Then what kind of man will you be looking for? A farmer?"

"Maybe. Or a cattle rancher. There's plenty of pioneer settlers in the territory who need wives. Next time you're in Bowden's Store, take a look at the board on the back wall. It's covered with ads. Men come down here to stake out a claim on a piece of land and think they're going to get rich, but it seldom works out that way. But that's another story. Anyway, some of them are bachelors, but some come down with their families. There aren't many doctors down here, and medicine is scarce, so if the wife dies in childbirth, as many of them do, or succumbs to one of the terrible tropical diseases, the man is left alone to take care of his homestead and his family. I like children; I really do. I wouldn't mind marrying a man who had a ready-made family."

"I–I'm sure you would make a very good mother," Margaret said, being unable to think of an appropriate comment. "I wish you success in your choice, Lucy."

"I'm going out for a stroll," Lucy told her. "I don't like to go outside until the sun goes down. It's not good for your skin, you know." She stood and smoothed her black skirt. "Would you care to go along? It's very pleasant until the mosquitoes come out and start to bite."

"Thank you, Lucy. Perhaps I'll join you another evening, but not tonight."

Margaret watched Lucy amble out of the room. *Poor Lucy! I cannot imagine a woman coming all the way down here to this desolate territory to marry a man she didn't even know,* Margaret thought, before she was struck by the startling realization that she had almost done the same thing. At least, her situation would have been very similar, for she was now able to admit to herself that she had scarcely known Allen Fairchild. She realized now that she had wanted to marry him for all the wrong reasons. But still she grieved for him and for the terrible waste of his life.

❧

As word spread among the military wives, the demand for Margaret's bonnets escalated. The women who could afford them scooped them up so fast that Margaret scarcely had enough of them left in her trunk to cover her own head.

Three weeks had passed since the *Windsong* sailed out of Tampa Bay, and still Margaret had heard nothing from Mikal Lee. Perhaps he had forgotten her the moment his ship had pulled away from the Tampa docks.

Although her coins were multiplying at a satisfying rate, Margaret knew that there was no way she could replenish her supply of hats. The very fact that they were so unattainable was what had created such a great demand for them.

She was rather handy with a needle and thread and entertained the thought of making more hats, but the fabrics available from Bowden's General Store were sturdy and plain, not at all the quality she would need to satisfy her discriminating clientele.

She looked in her trunk and eyed the last two bonnets left from her bridal trousseau. If she sold those two, she would have to go bareheaded herself. With the trunk lid still open, she allowed her eyes to travel over her beautiful, handmade gowns, expertly crafted of the finest fabrics in all of Savannah.

She calculated that just one gown would make half a dozen bonnets if she cut carefully. But to cut up her lovely dresses would be like cutting off part of her own body. Unthinkable! There had to be some other answer.

She ran her hands over the soft silks and laces, caressing their folds with her fingers. Tears dropped into the trunk and landed on a pale, blue velvet skirt, creating dark polka-dots on the plush pile of the fabric. She closed the lid quickly. "No! I won't cut up my pretty dresses! They're all that I have left to remind me of the life I left behind."

But next morning, as soon as she finished breakfast, she went upstairs to her room and selected a silk lavender afternoon dress from her trunk. Its leg-o'-mutton sleeves would be much too hot for this tropical climate anyway, she rationalized. She stretched its wide skirts across her bed and held her scissors in the air. *God, help me!* And it startled her to realize that she was praying again.

Her hands were shaking so that the blades made a rattling sound. *This will be like performing surgery on someone I love!* But gritting her teeth together, she made the first long slash into the soft, lustrous folds. Swish! As the silk gave way beneath her hands, her heart skipped a beat, but after the first painful gash, her task gradually became easier, and she began to slice into the fabric with a great deal more assurance than she actually felt.

All morning she worked, measuring and cutting, saving every scrap and sliver of cloth as a possible source of trimming. By the time she went downstairs for dinner, her back ached, but she was proud that she had cut out six bonnets. She would have to figure a way to trim each of them differently, because no two women from Fort Brooke would want to go out in matching bonnets.

The gentlemen boarders did not appear at the table for the noon meal. "They aren't able to eat dinner with us during the week because they can't leave their offices until evening," Miss Priscilla explained. "Each morning I pack them each a sack of food to take along."

Dinner was a simple meal of collard greens and corn pone. Margaret enjoyed Miss Priscilla's home-cooked meals, and she was particularly hungry today after her morning's work.

The Rosada sisters sat side by side, arguing about what colors should be used for the windmill quilt they were making. "I favor blue," Miss Hope declared. "Don't you like blue, Mrs. White?" she asked, trying to acquire an ally to support her choice before her sister voiced an opinion.

"Don't be ridiculous," Miss Charity said before Lucy could answer. "Blue would be all wrong with as many yellow and green pieces as we've put into the windmills. It has to be green, don't you think, Miss Porter?"

"I–I really like blue and green both. But, uh, pink is a very popular color this year. Perhaps you should think about using pink."

"Yes. Oh, yes," Lucy agreed. "Pink would be a lovely choice!"

The sisters looked at each other with raised eyebrows, smiled, and nodded, and Margaret and Lucy heaved simultaneous sighs of relief.

Margaret hurried through her meal, and as soon as she could

gracefully do so, she excused herself, anxious to return to her work.

Her room was a shambles! Lavender silk was stacked in six piles on her bed, and threads and ravels littered the floor. The remains of her once-beautiful gown lay in a pitiful heap in the corner. Margaret tried not to look at the mound of shredded lavender silk, turning her chair so that it faced toward the window.

With needle and thread, she began to stitch the first bonnet and was delighted as she watched it begin to take shape beneath her hands. She had never made a bonnet before, but she found the task quite pleasurable, and by the time the afternoon light began to fade, she had completed the basic framework of three bonnets. All that was left for her to do now was the trimming.

Tomorrow she would walk to the village and see what Bowden's General Store had to offer in the way of laces and ribbons. And she could clip the bows and satin rosettes from what was left of her dissected lavender gown, and hem some strips of the fabric to use for ruffles. She felt the exciting challenge of giving each bonnet an individual look entirely different from the others. In her mind's eye, she could see them already, so pretty that she might want to keep one for herself!

Much later, as she lay in bed thinking about her bonnets and the coins she was accumulating, she felt the sense of satisfaction that comes with overcoming a seemingly immovable obstacle. Just a few weeks ago, she could see no possible way out of her troubles, and now things seemed to be falling into place.

Mikal had told her that with God, all things were possible. He had asked her to turn all of her problems over to God, assuring her that He would show her the way. But she hadn't really turned things over to God, had she? Just because she had offered a few prayers didn't mean that she had put God in control of her life. Mikal Lee had told her that he would be praying for her, too. Could God possibly have a hand in her recent achievements?

God, if you're listening, I'm still not sure I'm ready to give up being in control of my own affairs, but if You're in any way responsible for helping me get on with my life, then I just want to thank You!

Night shadows danced across her bedroom wall, and Margaret imagined that they were hands held out to welcome her. As sleep claimed her body, she drifted on a dream out to meet them.

six

Margaret was elbow deep in green taffeta when a knock sounded on her bedroom door.

"Miss Porter?"

Margaret did not welcome the interruption. It was difficult to stop in the middle of measuring a brim for an exact fit to the bonnet she had just cut out. She could not afford to make mistakes with her dwindling supply of fabric. "Just a moment, please," she mumbled, trying not to release the pins she had caught between her lips. She recognized the voice of Isabelle, the Spanish maid who helped Miss Priscilla in the dining room. Whatever could she want with her at this time of the morning?

She put her pins in the little dish on the chest of drawers and laid her scissors beside them. Opening her door just a crack, she peeped out. "Yes, Izzy, what is it?"

"A gentleman to see you, miss. He is in the parlor waiting to see you."

"For me? Are you sure? Who is he?" Perhaps one of the officers from Fort Brooke wanted a new bonnet to surprise his wife. Margaret was having a hard time keeping up with the increasing demand.

"He did not say his name, but he is the same man that brought you here."

"The—who? Oh, my!" Margaret closed the door, and then remembering her manners, opened it again and called after the retreating maid, "Thank you, Izzy. Tell the gentleman I'll be right down!"

Margaret ran a brush over her hair and pinched her cheeks to bring out their color. She fluffed out her skirts and smoothed them and hurried down the stairs to see if Mikal Lee had really returned!

He stood when she entered the parlor, and she was so glad to see him that she almost rushed across the room to embrace him. Coming to her senses, she remembered her manners; and she also remembered that she had heard nothing from him for over six weeks. She matched his smile and held her hands outstretched. "Mikal! I am so glad to see you again. It's been a very long time. I was not sure that you even still remembered me."

He gripped her small hands in his big, rough ones and gazed into her face. The earnest look in his dark blue eyes made it impossible for her to doubt his sincerity when he said, "Margaret, there has not been a day since I left here that I haven't thought of you. I would have been back much sooner, but we ran into a terrible storm in the Gulf of Mexico. Fortunately, God was with us and we did not lose any men, but the *Windsong* suffered major damage. We had to put in at St. Marks for repairs before we could come the rest of the way. But enough of my troubles. How are you? I've been very concerned about you."

The nearness of him almost took her breath away, but she tried to mask her excitement. "Concerned? Whatever for, Mikal? I am perfectly well, thank you."

"Then are you ready to go back to Savannah with me when we sail out of here tomorrow?"

"Tomorrow?" Just when she felt so happy to see him again, she found that he was leaving. "I–I thought you would stay a few days as you did before."

"We're already two weeks behind schedule in delivering our load of cotton to the New York mills. We can't afford any more delays. I know it isn't much notice, Margaret, but I brought a carriage, and I'll help you get ready to leave."

"Leave? Oh, no, Mikal, I'm not leaving. I'm staying here. I've been—oh, there is so much to tell you. I don't know where to begin. And I want to ask a big favor of you, too. Why don't you dismiss the carriage and go for a walk with me? I promise not to keep you long, but we do need to talk."

"Indeed we do," Mikal agreed. He went outside to talk to the driver, and Margaret went upstairs to fetch her bonnet and reticule.

Because the morning sun was almost halfway across the sky, she decided to take along her yellow silk parasol. She left her partially finished bonnets on the bed, locked her door, and hurried down the stairs.

"Izzy, I may not return in time for dinner. Could you save a little snack for me in case I'm late getting back?"

The little maid smiled and winked. "I will do better than that. If you will wait just a few minutes, I will pack your dinner in a sack, and I'll put in a little extra in case you decide to share it with your gentleman friend."

When Mikal returned, Izzy handed him a croker sack. "This is for when you and the señorita get hungry," she said. Her black eyes twinkled, and a smile spread across her caramel-colored face. "Now, you take good care of Miss Porter, you hear?"

"Indeed I shall try," Mikal promised. "Thank you very much."

Margaret, holding her parasol in one hand and her reticule in the other, led the way down the porch steps. She opened the parasol and held it at an angle that at once shielded her face from the sun but allowed Mikal to see her face.

This time they walked in the opposite direction of the village, where the road was bordered by palmettos, thorny bushes, and a sprinkling of wildflowers. The air was fresh and clean, and the cloudless sky promised a morning without rain.

"Mikal," she began, "there are reasons why I cannot return

to Savannah just yet, but I need your help."

"I'll do whatever I can to help you, Margaret. You should know that by now."

"Yes. Well, I guess I do, and I deeply appreciate all that you have done for me already. I don't know what I would have done without your help. And I don't want to keep imposing on your friendship. I'll try to make this the last favor I'll ask of you, but it's a big one."

"I should be very disappointed if it's the last, but let's hear it. What is it you need?"

"I've written a letter to my father in Savannah. The mail in and out of here is so undependable that I thought perhaps you might deliver it for me on your way north."

"Of course. That isn't such a big favor. I'll be glad to see that he gets it."

"But there's more," she continued. "I'll be expecting a reply. If you could wait while he gets the. . .um. . .that is, while he writes something to send back to me, it would be much safer than trusting it to the mail."

"Of course. I can do that." They walked along in silence for a few minutes while Mikal gave the matter some thought. Suddenly he took her arm and drew her to a stop on the side of the road. "Margaret, if it's money that you need, I can help you. You can go back on the *Windsong* today and make payment for your passage later. I'll speak to my partner, and I'm sure he'll agree to the arrangement. I don't like to leave you down here in the territory alone. It's much too dangerous for a lady."

Margaret bristled. "I'm not as helpless as you may think, Mikal. In fact, I–I've become involved in a little business here, and I don't feel I should leave just now."

Mikal scowled. What kind of business could Margaret be involved in? He knew that there were crooks and charlatans who sold everything from useless swampland to worthless inventions. Anything to make unsuspecting investors part with their gold. He did not know how much money Margaret had brought from Savannah, but her clothing gave evidence that she came from a wealthy family.

He could not force her to return home. Perhaps the next best thing, then, would be to contact her father as she requested. He would warn her father of the dangers Margaret faced and urge him to bring her back home.

"If you won't come with me, then I will do as you ask, Margaret. Give me the letter and tell me how to reach your father, and I will bring you his reply as soon as I come this way again."

Margaret felt a warm sense of security in Mikal's presence. She hated the thought of his leaving again. "How long before you return?" she asked, trying not to let her voice betray how much she really cared.

"That depends on a lot of things. Weather, economy, the number of people booking passage, and their needs, to mention a few."

They came to a grassy clearing alongside the road, shaded by massive, spreading oaks. Moss hung from the branches like filmy gray curtains and swayed in the gentle breeze. "Would you like to stop for a little snack?" Margaret suggested.

Mikal jumped at the chance. "A great idea! I'll have to admit that I've walked up an appetite."

Margaret spread her full skirts across the prickly grass and sandy earth, and Mikal sprawled on the ground beside her. His gaze revealed what his words did not—that he was not nearly so interested in the food as he was in his lovely companion.

Margaret munched on a pimento cheese sandwich, spread on thick slices of Miss Priscilla's own sourdough bread, and let her thoughts wander.

She was aware of a growing magnetism between herself and Mikal Lee that she must somehow find a way to resist. She had almost made a foolish mistake once before by letting her heart rule over her head. But she was older and wiser now. Even in the short span of a few weeks, she felt that she had matured well beyond her twenty years. Mikal was a sailor. He was a kind man who probably had a list of men and women all up and down both coasts whom he cared about and tried to help. She must be careful not to attach too much importance to their growing friendship.

Mikal was silently engrossed in his own thoughts. He shifted his weight and propped his chin in his hand to get a clearer view of her face. Margaret Porter was unlike any woman he had ever met before. She looked so vulnerable sitting there in the grass, her long, dark hair blown carelessly about her face. And she seemed to possess an inner beauty that was equal to her nearly flawless physical beauty. It would be so easy to fall in love with her, but there were so many reasons why that would be all wrong.

First and foremost, Margaret was not yet an avowed Christian. If he ever did marry, Mikal knew that he would choose a woman who was willing to work beside him to establish a Christian home for their family, and Margaret Porter did not fit that description.

But then, there was little likelihood that she could ever love him anyway. She was in mourning for the soldier she had loved and lost. Some women never recovered from a shock like that, and he was not willing to compete with the ghost of Allen Fairchild.

This was all just as well, he thought, because he had already decided long ago that he would probably never marry anyone at all. His life was with the sea, and a sailor's life was not compatible with marriage and a family. He knew that well enough, having only vague recollections of his own father. A wife and children deserved more than a part-time husband and father.

Margaret had already begun to pick up the scraps left from their snack. "I promised not to keep you long," she said. "I know you must get back to your ship, and I don't want to detain you."

The walk back to the boardinghouse seemed all too short. Their silence gave evidence that each was absorbed with sober thoughts. When they reached the boardinghouse steps, Mikal said, "I'll wait here while you get your letter. But Margaret, I'm going to ask a favor of you in return."

"What do you mean?"

"Go get your letter. I'll tell you about it when you return."

Margaret scurried up the steps to her room. She pulled her father's letter from her dresser drawer and held it close to her heart. *Please, God, let this letter reach my father, and let him send me word of his forgiveness.* Carrying the letter in her hand, she locked her bedroom door and started back down the stairs. What kind of favor would Mikal ask in return? If he wanted money, she had a nice little cache, and she did not think it unreasonable that he might ask for compensation. After all, her request was going to cause him some little inconvenience, and he deserved to be compensated.

She met him on the porch and handed him the letter. "The directions to my father's house are written on the outside, Mikal. I don't think you'll have any problem finding it, and he will gladly pay you for the delivery."

Mikal took the slightly scented pink letter from her hand and tucked it into his jacket pocket. Then, reaching into his inside pocket, he pulled out a small black book. "Now it's my turn," he said. "I have a favor to ask of you."

Margaret was already opening her little reticule, pushing her fingers inside to extract a few of her gold and silver coins. "Yes, of course—"

"I want you to promise me that you'll read some of this each day," he said, pressing the book into her hands. "This is the

New Testament. I'd like for you to read a portion of it each day. Read as much of it as you can before I return, so that we can talk about it together."

"A Bible? That's the favor you're asking of me?"

"Yes. Will you promise to read it while I'm gone?"

Margaret slipped the strings of her reticule over her wrist to free both of her hands. She held the book and opened the leather binding to the first page. Written in black ink, carefully penned words danced across the page. *To Margaret from Mikal, May 1836.* Beneath his name, he had written: *Commit thy way unto the Lord; trust also in him; and he shall bring it to pass. Psalm 37:5.*

Margaret pressed the book to her heart. "Thank you, Mikal. You're such a good, kind man. I promise to read a bit of this every day. But, Mikal, that's *all* I can promise. Just. . .just don't expect too much from me." In the broad light of day, with all the world looking on, she leaned forward and kissed him lightly on the cheek before she turned and ran back into the house.

seven

On the evening of Mikal's departure, Margaret felt a tremendous letdown, and that letdown feeling disturbed her greatly. How could she miss so terribly someone she had barely come to know? Remembering that she had recently been pledged to another man, Margaret decided that she must be a very fickle person. And as such, she did not deserve anyone as fine as Mikal Lee. Her self-esteem plummeted to an all-time low.

In the privacy of her room, Margaret lowered her window shades and readied herself for bed. Outside, a light rain brought darkness earlier than usual and made gentle taps against her windowpane. She poured water into her washbowl and sponged the dust from her body before slipping into her chemise and falling onto her bed. In the distance, she could hear steamboat whistles and thought again of Mikal, who was doubtless bouncing over the high seas by now.

Only then did she remember her promise to him. Mikal had asked her to read each day from the New Testament he had given her. Margaret appreciated his thoughtfulness, and she fully intended to keep her promise, but tonight she was very tired. She would begin her readings tomorrow.

Lying quietly in the darkness, her conscience held sleep at bay. She had made a bargain with Mikal, and she was certain he would keep his part of it. The least she could do in return was to keep hers.

She dragged herself from the comfort of her bed and fumbled in the dark for her candle. By the flickering glow of a single flame, she opened her new book to the first chapter and began to read.

All those *begats* were surely not very interesting. She yawned and rubbed her eyes. But then she came to the verses that told about the birth of Jesus. These words were not exactly new to her, but she had pushed them into the inner recesses of her mind for so long that they had almost been forgotten. The farther she read, the more interested she became. Only when her candle began to sputter in its own melted wax did Margaret realize that she had read six exciting chapters and yearned to read on. Tomorrow she would ask Miss Priscilla for a new candle, and if she refused, she would buy one for herself at Bowden's General Store.

≈

Over the next few weeks, Margaret continued to turn out bonnets as fast as her fingers could fashion them. Although her reticule was bulging with coins, her supply of fabric was rapidly diminishing. She had only two dresses left. If she cut these up and turned them into bonnets, what would she wear to cover her own body?

When she had first arrived in Tampa, she had turned up her nose at the simple frocks the local women wore, but now she could see the practicality of them. The clothes she wore daily all bore watermarks around the bottom where she had tried to sponge away the inevitable dust that clung to their hemlines. Today when she went to the market, she would see about purchasing a calico dress for herself.

She wished that she had asked Mikal to bring her some stylish fabrics and trims from Savannah—or better yet, from New York! But on second thought, when Mikal came back with news from her father, she might never have to worry about making bonnets again! She could return to Savannah and become a pampered debutante again. That's what she wanted, wasn't it? Then why did her stomach turn upside down every time she thought of giving up her present lifestyle and returning to her old one?

Summer sun streamed through her bedroom window, and Margaret knew that very soon the heat would make her walk to the village unbearable. She wrapped the yellow bonnet she had just finished yesterday in one of her petticoats to keep it clean and packed it carefully into her sack. Meli had special-ordered it, and Margaret was sure she would be pleased. Tiny yellow roses bordered the brim, with green satin leaves tucked between the petals.

She would always be grateful to Meli and Katherine, who had not only been her first customers but had spread the word of Margaret's bonnets to all of their friends, so that she now had a hard time keeping up with their demands. Almost all of her designs now were made to order, sold before they were even sewn.

As Margaret drew near to the village, she noticed that almost no women were on the street today, and men stood in serious clusters waving their hands and talking. She continued on to the corner of the steps leading into the general store and stood in the shade of the porch to watch for Meli. This was the spot where she usually met her customers, but today Meli was nowhere to be seen. Perhaps she was running late this morning. Margaret decided to go inside the store and look at their supply of dresses while she waited.

Margaret chose a simple cotton frock made of brown checked gingham, cut with a square neckline and a full skirt that ended in a wide flounce. Then she purchased a five-yard piece of lavender dimity print sprigged with clusters of violets and green vines and leaves. This would make up into a cool dress that she could wear all summer. She also purchased enough unbleached muslin to make a pinafore to wear over her dresses to protect them from soil. She smiled, remembering her earlier firm resolve never to own such simple clothing. Now she looked forward with pleasure to the comfort and practicality they would offer her.

She counted out her coins on the counter and looked around the store for her friend. Again, she could not help but notice the scarcity of women this morning. "Mrs. Bowden, I was hoping to see my friend Meli. Have you seen her in the store this morning?"

"Ain't she one of them ladies from Fort Brooke?"

"Yes, that's the one. She was supposed to pick up a bonnet from me today."

"Then I reckon you ain't heard the news." When Margaret arched her eyebrows in question, the old lady continued, "They was another Injun raid yesterday 'bout dark, right outside of town. Some soldiers was returnin' to the base and got ambushed. They was a lot of bloodshed, and I hear the officers is all sending their womenfolk back home till things quiets down a mite. They say it's jist too dangerous around here right now. They's been a lot of outlaws roamin' these woods, too. Me and Ezekiel jist tries to stay inside the store and mind our own business."

"Oh, my! That's scary! Do you have any idea where I might find my friend today? I need to see her before she leaves town."

"Honey, I 'spect they done left already, or if they ain't, they soon will be. Whatcha got? One of your fancy bonnets fer her? Lemme see!"

Margaret unwrapped the yellow bonnet and handed it to the storekeeper. Mrs. Bowden ran her rough, gnarled fingers over the smooth fabric. "My, ain't that the prettiest thing you ever did see? I'd shore like to have one like that for myself."

"I could make you one," Margaret said hopefully. "Any kind you would like."

"Well, I'd like one jist like this, but I reckon it wouldn't be too practical. And Ezekiel would plumb die if I spent the kind of money you git fer these things, but it shore is pretty."

"I'll tell you what I'll do, Mrs. Bowden. If you will hold this bonnet for Meli and give it to her next time she stops in, I'll make you a bonnet from the remnants I have left after I cut out my new lavender dimity dress."

The old lady smiled a toothless grin. "Now won't that be grand? I'll take real good care of this here yeller one, and if your friend don't show up, I'll find somebody else to sell it to, and that's a fact."

Margaret asked the question she posed every week. "Has Mr. Bowden found anyone interested in buying my pearls?"

"Well, yes and no," Mrs. Bowden replied. "Last week they was a gent in here that took a real likin' to 'em. Didn't even quibble about the price, but when he went to pay, he tried to pay in that-there paper money. Now you know them shinplasters ain't worth nothin'. Ezekiel warn't born yesterday. He told that dandy to come back when he had some gold to offer. But you jist wait, honey. One of these days, one of them officers from Fort Brooke is gonna come in here alookin' fer something special to give his lady, and your pretty pearls will be jist the thing that'll please him."

"Thank you, Mrs. Bowden. I'll try to finish your bonnet by next week."

The woman clapped her splotched hands together in delight. "I can't hardly wait! Would you be awantin' anything else today?"

Margaret rubbed her chin and thought for a few moments. "Let me have two more of those tallow candles and a spool of white thread."

Margaret paid for her purchases and started toward home. Still she saw few women or children on the streets. Were the streets of Tampa village really becoming so dangerous, or was it just the summer heat that kept them all indoors? If the officers all sent their wives away, who would be left to buy Margaret's bonnets? She had enough money to last for a while, but what would she do when her supply ran out?

Oh, how much longer will it be before Mikal Lee returns?

&

As the *Windsong* tacked into Tampa Bay, Mikal stood on her deck and tried to summon the words he would use to tell Margaret the heartbreaking news. How would she react to this latest tragedy in her life?

He had tried to offer her comfort when Allen Fairchild had died, but how could he hope to help her survive two such losses within so short a span of time?

Mikal knew of only one source for the magnitude of comfort Margaret would need in the days ahead. If only she would turn *to* God in her times of trial instead of turning *away* from Him, He would surely lift her up and help her bear her burdens. But Mikal remembered how angrily she had lashed out at God when Allen was killed. Would this latest news drive an even deeper wedge between Margaret and the Lord?

If only he could bring her just a little good news to temper the bad, he would find his job easier. But Cedric Porter had not only taken his own life, he had left behind mounds of unpaid bills so that his creditors were lined up to collect any money derived from the sale of his properties. The only thing that Mikal had been able to bring for Margaret was a note from her father, and he had even had to argue with the barristers over that. Mikal wondered whether the contents of this note would help to soften the blow or only make it worse. The note was still unread, secured with her father's wax seal. Mikal thanked God that the investigating officers had finally agreed to allow her that last small semblance of privacy and dignity.

Mikal pulled the note from his jacket pocket and turned it over in his hands. He wished that he knew its contents. He hoped that the words would not heap a burden of guilt on poor Margaret. She had all the sorrow she could handle without adding guilt to her grief.

Although Mikal had previously urged her to return to Savannah, he was now glad that she was far away from the ugly accusations and legal entanglements her father had left as her legacy. Had Margaret been aware of her father's gambling compulsion, or would this be just one more thing heaped on her pile of misery?

He longed to see her; he had missed her so. Standing on the deck with the salty spray stinging his face, he could still imagine the way she had looked that first time when he saw her standing on the deck, the ocean wind swirling her dark hair around her face.

Dear Father, help me to find words that will soften this shock for Margaret. Let me be Your instrument to bring some good out of all this tragedy about to be revealed to her. Give me strength, Lord, because I know I can't handle this alone.

As the ship eased against its moorings, Mikal whispered his final *Amen* and began preparations to disembark. What he had earlier thought would be a day of joy for him had now turned into a day of utter despair.

eight

Margaret sat on the porch in a cane-backed rocking chair, her Bible spread across her lap. The midsummer heat had been stifling in her room, but now a cool breeze lifted the hair from the back of her neck and dried the perspiration on her forehead. The air was fresh, blushed by the soft haze that follows sunset.

The days were growing longer now, and for an hour or two after supper each night, Margaret was able to read without the aid of her candle. By sitting on the porch, she could extend that time by as much as half an hour.

She had read through the Gospels, and she was now well into Romans. Begun as a chore performed to fulfill a promise, her daily reading had now grown to be the favorite event of her day.

Although she had not yet come to the point of making a full, personal commitment, she had begun to give the matter some serious thought. She just wasn't sure she could live up to its demands. Being a Christian was well and good for people like Mikal, but in spite of all that she had read in the Bible, Margaret found it hard to believe that God could accept someone who had turned against Him and lashed out at Him as she had.

And there was another point that gave her some difficulty—the part about forgiving others. She still had not been able to find it in her heart to forgive the red savages who had murdered Allen and other fine men like him, and she did not think she ever would.

With her eyes focused on the fine print of her Testament,

she did not see Mikal's approach until he stood at the bottom porch step.

"Mikal!" She almost tripped on her skirts as she hurried to meet him, but when she was halfway down the steps, she realized by the expression on his face that something was terribly wrong. She looked at his sober, strained countenance, and her stomach did a flip-flop. She was not at all sure she wanted to hear this news he had come to tell her. Had her father completely disowned her because she had gone against his wishes? Did he refuse, not only to send her money, but to even welcome her back into his home? "Mikal, what is it? What is the matter?"

Mikal wrapped her in his arms. "Margaret, I have bad news. Let's go inside where we can talk."

When he released her, she reeled and stumbled against him. He put an arm around her waist and supported her up the steps and into the parlor. The drapes were drawn so that the room was dark and musty. Again he drew her into his arms and told her the whole sad story of how he had gone to her home, talked with the barristers and investigating officers, and discovered the devastating news of her father's death.

"The only thing they would allow me to bring you is this note, probably the last thing that your father ever wrote." Mikal continued to hold her while she soaked his shirt with her tears.

Trembling as though it were mid-January instead of a warm day in June, Margaret pushed him away and reached with trembling fingers for the letter.

"Shall I light a candle so that you can see to read?"

"No, not yet. I–I don't think I can bear to read it just yet. I'll save it for later. Right now I, well, uh, I just want to—Mikal— would you pray for me?"

Her startling request caught Mikal by surprise. Out of such a dark moment, her words were like a ray of sunshine to his heart. While God was closing one door, he seemed to be opening another. "Of course I will."

He took her hands in his and dropped his head. "Dear heavenly Father. . ."

As Mikal's strong, deep voice resonated in the high-ceilinged keeping room, Margaret's sobs began to subside. At last, when Mikal said "Amen" and lifted his head, she raised her reddened eyes to look into his face. "Thank you so much. I know what a difficult job this must have been for you, coming here to bring me such sad news. And I wish that there was some way I could tell you how much your friendship means to me. . ."

"Margaret, you don't have to. . ."

"But just now, Mikal, if you don't mind, I think I want to be alone for a while."

"Are you sure? Because I'll stay here with you for as long as you need me."

"Thank you, but no. I want to go upstairs and read my letter, and then I'm going to read my Bible and pray. The Lord will be with me, and I will be fine."

Mikal said, "It seems almost sinful for me to call this a moment of joy, Margaret, and it doesn't take away any of my sorrow for your grief, but you've just made me a very happy man. I'll respect your wishes and leave you alone for now, but I'll be back to see you in the morning."

"Look, Mikal, I know what you must be thinking. But remember what I told you last time we were together, and don't expect too much from me. I've come a long way, but there are still a lot of things I have to work out yet. I'm not sure that I ever will."

"It's all right, Margaret. I have a lot of patience, but God has even more."

⁂

The *Windsong* stayed moored at the docks of Tampa Bay for

three days, unloading supplies brought from the northern markets and refueling the ship.

On the morning of the third day, Mikal came to the boardinghouse early and asked Margaret if she felt up to a small picnic in the clearing where they had stopped once before. "I know you have a heavy heart and don't feel like making long-range plans, but we do need to talk about your future before I sail."

"Yes. Yes, I think I would like that," Margaret said. "I have things I want to discuss with you, too."

Izzy packed them a bag of food, and they set out on foot along the road that led away from the village. Soon the road became a narrow, winding trail through tall pines, majestic oaks, and palmettos. The early morning air was pleasantly cool, and the silence that lay between them was comfortable, the way it can only be between close friends.

When they came to the familiar clearing, Mikal picked a bouquet of wildflowers and handed them to Margaret. "Flowers for milady," he said, bowing in mock formality.

"Why, thank you, sir." Margaret accepted the bouquet and curtsied. Then, laughing, she knelt in the tender green grass and arranged her skirts around her.

Mikal slumped down beside her and reached for her hand. It was good to hear her laughter again, even though he knew that she carried a heavy pain in her heart. "Margaret, I wanted to come here today so that we could have a very serious conversation. I know that my suggestion is going to sound rather abrupt under the circumstances, but from everything I've heard, Tampa is getting to be a much too dangerous place for a lady. I want you to consider moving away from here."

Margaret's green eyes widened with surprise. "But Mikal, I have nowhere else to go. You yourself told me about the impossible situation in Savannah. Going back there now would only mean trouble for me. I have my bonnet business here in Tampa, and I have no intention of moving away."

"But you told me yesterday that your bonnets weren't selling as well since the officers sent their wives away from Fort Brooke. For all we know, those women may never return to this wild and lawless land, and who could blame them? And the poor people of the village don't have the kind of money your fancy bonnets are worth."

"Lately I've been sewing sunbonnets from the cheap calico I can buy at the general store, but you're right. I'm only able to ask a dollar for each one, and they take almost as much time to make as the fancier ones. The women insist that I attach a bavolet at the back to protect their necks from the sun, and that takes extra fabric as well as time. Don't you think the military wives will be returning to Tampa soon?"

"Margaret, Andrew Jackson is determined to move all the Indians to Oklahoma, and the tension between the Seminoles and the army is only going to intensify. This area is no fit place for a lady. I have what I think is a better suggestion."

"I'm certainly willing to listen." In truth, Margaret wished that she could listen to Mikal all day long. Listening to his tender voice, watching the kindness reflected on his face made her wish that he would never leave. But of course that was one wish that she knew could never come true.

"When the *Windsong* leaves Tampa tomorrow, we'll be headed for a town in the northwestern part of the territory called Apalachicola. That's where we go to pick up the bales of cotton brought down the river by farmers from Alabama and Georgia. Apalachicola is one of the busiest ports in the territory, and I think your bonnets would be much in demand by the ladies there. You could leave with me on the *Windsong* when we sail out of here tonight, and when we get to Apalachicola, I'll have a few days in port to help you get settled. I have friends there who could help you, too, and I think you'd be much safer and happier there."

"But Mikal, I can't just leave tonight. I—I'm not ready to make such a decision! So much is happening so fast! I have to have time to think about this."

Mikal chewed on a blade of grass and wrinkled his brow. "Margaret, I really wish I could convince you to come away from this place right now, tonight! But I can understand your reluctance. I've heaped a lot on your plate already this week. But if you won't go with me now, at least promise me you'll give this idea some serious thought while I'm gone. I'll be coming back here in a few weeks. I'll stop by to see you on my way north to deliver the cotton bales to the textile mills in New York. It will likely be a couple of months before I come back through Tampa on my way to Apalachicola again."

"I–I'll think about it," she promised. "Now we'd better eat our food and start back. I mustn't keep you here when you have so much work to do."

Although the biscuits left over from breakfast were now cold, they were still high and light. Spread with Miss Priscilla's homemade guava jam, Mikal declared that they were better than anything he had eaten on board the *Windsong* since leaving the last port.

Margaret's appetite had been practically nonexistent since she'd received the news of her father's death, and this was the first food that had passed her lips since yesterday noon, when she had eaten a few bites of Izzy's chicken noodle soup. But as she began to nibble at one of the sweetened biscuits, she found herself enjoying it.

"Must you go, Mikal?" she asked, wiping her lips on one of the linen napkins Izzy had thought to include. She dreaded the long weeks that stretched ahead without his company. Then, embarrassed by her aggressive plea, she answered her own question. "Yes, of course, I know that you must!"

"Let me pray with you before I leave."

"I—I'm not sure that I want you to do that, Mikal. I don't want to encourage you to expect more of me than I can deliver. I told you that I've come a long way, but I think you should know that I still hold a lot of hate in my heart."

"Hate is destructive, Margaret. It's a heavy burden that only hurts the person who does the hating. Can't you find it in your heart to forgive whoever it is that you hate so much?"

"Indians!" She spit the word out like a mouthful of bitter medicine. "I hate them all! The Indians are evil people, and no, I can't find it in my heart to forgive them for their barbaric actions."

"Wait, Margaret. You've got it all wrong! To say that all Indians are evil is like saying that all dogs bite. There are many Indians who are fine men, honorable and good. Then, of course, there are some bad ones, too, just as there are bad white men. But take a minute to look at it from their point of view. These people are being driven from their homeland. They're trying to hold on to a land they believe to be their own. Killing is wrong, but it isn't fair to hold a prejudice against an entire race because of the actions of a few."

"Mikal Lee, how can you sit here and defend them after what they've done? It isn't just about Allen, you know. They massacred his entire company, and they're still riding about, ravaging the countryside. If God is so good, then how can He allow things like this to happen?" Her voice rose to a frantic pitch.

"Margaret, God isn't running a puppet show! He doesn't just pull all our strings to make us move. He allows us to make our own decisions. Sometimes we make bad ones, but at least we're free to choose." He reached for her hand, but she jerked it away from him. "I'm so sorry I've upset you," he apologized. "Perhaps we should be starting back. My ship sets sail in a few hours."

Together they gathered up the scraps of their picnic and

began their walk along the trail back to the boardinghouse. This time the silence that lay between them was filled with a million unspoken words.

nine

In the weeks following Mikal's last visit, Margaret had plenty of time to contemplate her choices for the future, and none of them gave her much joy.

The one thing of which she was certain was that she could never return to face her friends in Savannah. That would be humiliating as well as heartbreaking. Besides, there was nothing left for her there. Mikal had brought her the upsetting news that her father's creditors had seized all of his property and would likely expect her to make up the shortfall if she were to return. But her little stash of coins would not even begin to cover Cedric Porter's monumental debts. No, Margaret could not return to Savannah.

Her home now consisted of one small room in Miss Priscilla's Boardinghouse. As sparse as it might seem, it was now the one familiar spot in her world, and she was reluctant to give that up to move to a town with a name she could not even pronounce, let alone spell!

Yet Mikal's words kept echoing in her ears, and the longer she listened to them, the more sensible they became. Her bonnet business was almost at a standstill. What would she do when her present supply of money ran out? What did other decent women do to survive in the Florida Territory? She let her thoughts run over the list of women she knew.

Miss Priscilla, of course, ran her own thriving boardinghouse. Margaret had been told that Miss Priscilla had been born and reared in this house; her parents had come into the territory as pioneers. Margaret had no such legacy to fall back on.

She was not sure how the Rosada sisters derived the money for their keep, but they seemed to live very frugally. Miss Charity had told her once that their papa had been one of the early missionaries to the territory, but of course Hope had disputed that statement, saying that he was a farmer who used his spare time to preach the Gospel to the Indians and the white settlers. Whatever their background, the sisters had never divulged their source of income.

Lucy White received a small widow's pension from the army, but she planned to marry again as soon as she passed through her respectable period of mourning. Margaret certainly wasn't going to follow that path. So what other options did she have?

Mikal had predicted that her bonnet business would flourish in that coastal town with the strange name. It would take a great deal of courage to pull up her tenuous roots and move to a place she had never seen, but Margaret had done it once before, and with God's help, she would do it again. As soon as Mikal returned, she would tell him of her decision.

❧

By August, Margaret's reticule was almost empty. She still had two elegant gowns lying in the bottom of her trunk, along with her stiff, white crinolines. She was only too happy to forsake them in favor of her simple cotton frocks and muslin petticoats in the tropical heat of summer. She had even made herself a couple of muslin sunbonnets, saving her finer ones for what she hoped would be more prosperous days ahead.

Margaret had used her skill with a needle to make two new dresses and a pinafore apron for Miss Priscilla, thus earning two weeks of room and board, and Lucy had commissioned her to sew a blue gingham dress to end her period of mourning. Lucy would have preferred a more elegant fabric choice, but Bowden's supply was limited to the simple demands of their customers.

Every time Margaret heard the blast of a whistle from the docks, she hoped that it would signal the return of the *Windsong*, but it was mid-August before she saw Mikal again.

She had just washed her long, dark hair beneath the backyard pump, using a square cut from a block of Miss Priscilla's homemade lye soap. After she rinsed away the last traces of lather, she poured a mixture of vinegar and water through her hair, and then held her head beneath the stream of water while Izzie worked the handle of the old iron pump.

"Thank you, Izzie." She took the towel that Izzie held for her and sat on the kitchen steps to dry her hair in the sunshine.

"Good morning! Or is it afternoon already?"

Margaret's heart jumped at the sound of his voice. "Mikal!" Then her hands flew to her hair. "Oh, my! I must look a sight!"

Mikal thought that she looked like an angel, but he knew better than to tell her that. He remembered how soft she had felt in his arms last time he had come to see her, but he knew that it was only her grief that had allowed him to hold her against his chest and run his hands over her beautiful hair. With all the restraint he could muster, he said, "You look fine, Margaret. I am very glad to see you again."

He could not pull his eyes away from her. In the few weeks since he had last seen her, she had changed. Her simple gingham gown fell softly about her ankles in direct contrast to the wide, stiff skirts she usually wore, and the mass of damp hair that surrounded her face stripped away all of her city-girl pretenses and let her natural beauty shine through.

"I–I must run up to my room for a few minutes, but I'll be right back down." Before he could protest, she ran up the back steps, through the kitchen, and up the staircase to her room. How embarrassing to be caught in such disarray!

She changed quickly into her freshly ironed calico gown and forced a brush through the tangled mass of her hair. *Mikal is back! I mustn't keep him waiting! I don't want to waste a minute of the little time we have together!*

When she hurried down the stairs, he was waiting for her in the parlor, and she had to stifle her impulse to rush into his arms. She was so very happy to see him again! "You've been away for quite a long time."

"Too long. And I only have an hour."

Margaret's joy plummeted. *Only an hour!* And there was so much she wanted to say to him!

"The *Windsong* sails out again this afternoon. We're fully loaded with cotton, so there's no room for us to load anything else on the boat. We've only stopped long enough to take on two people who've booked passage to New York. As soon as we put their trunks on board, I'm afraid we have to pull anchor and sail. I'm detaining them as it is, but I had to see you to find out if you've made up your mind about moving."

"Yes, I have. It hasn't been an easy decision, but I see the sense in the plan you've outlined to me. I'll be ready when you come this way again."

Joy spread across his face like the rising of the morning sun. He reached out for her—he just could not help himself. Wrapping her in his arms, he half-expected her to protest, but when she yielded to his embrace, he whirled her around and lifted her off her feet.

"I've been so worried you wouldn't go," he said. "I'll be back for you as soon as we can unload our cotton and turn the *Windsong* around. Oh, Margaret, you've made me so happy!"

Margaret's cheeks were flushed and her head was reeling. She pushed away from him and tried to collect her thoughts. "What is the name of this town where I'm going?"

"Apalachicola! That's an Indian name that means 'Land Beyond.' " Seeing her flinch at the mention of Indians, he hastened to add, "It's a real progressive city. They have fancy dress balls and socials, and there's even an opera house. You'll likely have a thriving market for your fancy bonnets."

At the mention of her bonnets, Margaret's eyes opened wide in alarm. "Oh, but Mikal, I can't—that is, I have no elegant fabrics and trims left to make more bonnets, and I don't think the ladies in Apalachicola will want my calico sunbonnets."

Mikal thought for a few moments. "I think I can help you there, Margaret. If you can make up a list of the kinds and amounts of fabrics you need, I can buy them for you when I'm in New York. The trimmings, too. Just give me a list of everything you need, and I'll bring them back with me when I return. You'll be all ready to set up your new business when we get to Apalachicola."

"I don't know, Mikal. It sounds like it is all going to cost a great deal of money—more money than I have."

"I'd be willing to help you get started." When Mikal read her unspoken protest, he added before she had a chance to speak, "I've been looking for a wise investment for some of my funds, and this sounds like a good opportunity for me. Suppose we consider ourselves partners in this new business. When the profits start rolling in, we'll share them."

"Oh, it's all so frightening to me. Do you really think it will work?"

"I know it will," Mikal said. He pulled a scrap of paper and a stub of a pencil from his pocket. "We'd better get started on your list because it's almost time for me to go."

He jotted down the items as Margaret reeled them off. "I don't know what half this stuff is, but I suppose I can find someone in New York to help me."

"There's nothing there that's out of the ordinary, Mikal. Any person familiar with fabrics should be able to fill the order."

"Then that's about it, I guess, unless you can think of

anything else you might need."

Margaret shook her head. "That should be enough to keep me busy for a while, and if you need to make substitutions on any of it, feel free to do so. I'll just work with whatever you're able to bring me."

Mikal looked up at the sun and frowned. "It's getting late. As much as I hate to, I really must get back to the ship. Will you walk partway with me?"

As they strolled down the street side by side, Mikal took hold of her hand and was encouraged when she did not pull out of his grasp. In fact, he felt her fingers tighten around his.

"This is far enough," he told her. "I don't want you walking along the waterfront alone. Would you like me to get a carriage to take you home?"

"No, I'd rather walk," she said. Her eyes stung with unshed tears, and she fought to keep them back. She could hardly bear to see him leave again. "How long will it be before you return?"

"If we're blessed with good weather, I might make it back in four weeks. You can be sure that I'll come as quickly as I possibly can."

He turned to look down into her eyes and the sight of her took his breath away. Dark hair blew capriciously about her face in the late summer breeze, and the afternoon sun gave it an iridescent glow. Slipping his hands around her waist, he drew her to him and kissed her lightly on the lips. She did not pull away from him, but instead slipped her arms around his neck and entangled her fingers in his silky hair. "Oh, Mikal!"

She almost lost her balance when he pulled back from her, abruptly, as though the whole idea had been a terrible mistake, and without another word, he was gone.

Puzzled by his strange behavior, Margaret watched his retreating silhouette until she could see him no more. Would she ever understand that man? When he was completely beyond her sight, she turned and retraced her steps back to the boardinghouse she now called home.

ten

As Mikal's absence stretched into lonely weeks, Margaret had plenty of time to think about their strange relationship. She knew that for her he had become much more than a good friend, and her feelings for him ran much deeper than she had ever intended. And now, if things worked out as they planned, he was to become her business partner.

In her saner moments, Margaret knew that for Mikal, she was just one more girl on his long list of friends. Hadn't he told her himself of his many friends in Apalachicola? And no doubt, with his kind and generous nature and his gregarious personality, he had developed friendships all up and down both coasts.

She wanted to quell this senseless racing of her pulse every time he came near. Just thinking about him gave her a tingly feeling that she could not seem to repress. This wasn't love, of course. She had fooled herself once into thinking that she was in love with Allen Fairchild, when all she had really felt for him was an immature infatuation with his stunning good looks and his impressive military uniform. But during recent months, she had felt herself change from that silly girl into a mature woman. She was determined to keep a clear head and not let her heart run rampant again with foolish notions about love.

She should never have allowed that kiss beneath the oak tree. It had robbed her of her good sense and left her shaken. By now Mikal probably thought of her as an easy conquest. She had heard of women who were free with their kisses and even more, but she was certainly not one of them. She must make sure that Mikal understood that next time they met.

Four long weeks had passed, and still Margaret had heard nothing from Mikal Lee. Perhaps he had begun to have second thoughts about his rash offer to subsidize her new business venture.

Margaret was now beyond the point of turning back. She had finally sold her precious pearls for only a fraction of their worth—a mere pittance—but at least they gave her a little money to carry her through this move. She had already packed her few belongings in her trunk, and she had said her good-byes to her boardinghouse friends. She had even learned to spell Apalachicola!

The Rosada sisters had cried that evening when, sitting around the supper table, she had told them all she was leaving. "You're like one of the family," Miss Charity declared, dabbing at her eyes. "You're just like our little sister Faith, who died of malaria when she was just sixteen years old. Don't you think so, Sister?"

"She's not a bit like Faith," Miss Hope insisted, wiping the moisture from her own eyes. "Faith had lighter hair. Margaret is more like Mama's sister, Hannah."

"Well, no matter who you're like, I think you're making a big mistake, Margaret," Lucy White told her. "There are tons of men right here in the Tampa area and not nearly enough women to go around. Why, with your good looks, you could probably have your pick of the lot!"

Margaret blushed a deep scarlet. "It's not marriage I'm looking for, Lucy. I plan to set up a business for myself."

"If I may venture my humble opinion," Patrick said, "Mrs. White is quite right. Starting a new business is a man's work. I believe you would be much happier settling down with a good husband, keeping his house and raising his children without worrying your head over matters that are best left to menfolk."

Charles, sensing Margaret's growing anger, wisely resisted offering his own opinion, which did not differ greatly from Patrick's.

"Well, if you're all through offering your expert advice, can we go ahead and eat our supper before it gets cold? You've almost taken away my appetite," Margaret snapped.

Miss Priscilla pursed her lips and refrained from comment as she passed a bowl of hominy, followed by a square porcelain tureen of smothered chicken.

There was little conversation throughout the rest of the meal, the only noise coming from the clatter of silver against china. As soon as Margaret finished her supper, she pushed herself away from the table. "Please excuse me," she said crisply and marched up the stairs to her room.

She had enough misgivings of her own about the changes taking place in her life without adding to them from the opinions of the other boarders.

❧

Three days later, Mikal whistled his way up the sidewalk and appeared at the front door of Miss Priscilla's Boardinghouse.

Izzy was beside herself with excitement. She opened the door and eyed the carriage waiting at the end of the walk. "Oh, sir, come in. Just have a seat in the parlor, and I'll tell Miss Margaret you're here." She went bounding up the steps, calling at the top of her lungs, "Miss Margaret! Miss Margaret! Your gentleman friend is here!"

Margaret tried to still the sudden tremors that racked her body. Mikal was here at last, and her new adventure, for better or for worse, was about to begin! Her eyes circled the now familiar room. Once she left, there would be no turning back.

She opened the door a crack and saw Izzy literally jumping up and down with excitement. "Just tell him to have a seat in the parlor, Izzy. Tell the gentleman I will be down in a few minutes."

"Yes'm, I did that already. I'll go see if he wants tea."

Margaret closed the door and folded her arms across her chest, willing her heart to stop pounding. She yanked off the simple gingham dress she had put on this morning, along with her muslin pinafore, and stuffed them both into her trunk. Lifting her blue satin gown from the trunk, she began to dress with care. She stepped into her crinolines, slipped her dress over her head, and adjusted its redingote over her bouffant skirts. Using a button hook, she fastened her best leather shoes around her ankles and put her everyday ones in her trunk. She was beginning to feel like a real lady again!

She carried a small valise with the few things she would need during the trip, knowing that her trunk would be placed in the ship's storage until she arrived in Apalachicola. She tried to appear calm as she walked down the stairs.

Mikal, hearing her descending footsteps, rose from his chair in the parlor and stood at the bottom of the staircase to meet her. "Oh, Margaret, you do look lovely! Are you ready to leave, then?"

"I'm ready, Mikal. Is there someone who can help with my trunk?"

"I'll take care of everything. Let's get you settled in the hackney, and I'll ask the driver to help me bring down your trunk."

Margaret sat on the plush upholstery of the covered carriage and watched Mikal and the driver struggle to load her trunk on top. The Rosada sisters, Lucy White, Izzy, and even Miss Priscilla herself all stood on the porch to watch.

As they drove away, Margaret could hear Miss Hope sobbing aloud, and Lucy doing her best to quiet her. She held her lace-edged handkerchief out the window and waved to them until the horse-driven carriage turned the corner and erased them from her sight.

Margaret felt an unexpected tug at her heartstrings, as

though she were leaving her real blood family. These people had been her only family for the better part of a year, and now she knew that she would probably never see any of them ever again.

"Are you all right?" Mikal asked, sensing her distress.

"Yes, I'm fine," she assured him. "It's just all so new, and a little frightening, too."

He took her hand. "I'm sure that it must be. You've been through a great deal of stress since you left Savannah. But I'm also sure that you're doing the right thing now, Margaret. Trust me; you're going to like living in Apalachicola, and I—I'm going to be very happy to have you there."

"Were you able to find the supplies for my bonnets?"

Mikal's face broke into a broad grin. "I can hardly wait to unpack the boxes and show you what I brought. Velvets and satins, ribbons and laces, silk flowers, and even some of the newest hat forms to cover and trim. Your hats and bonnets are going to make you famous someday, Margaret Porter!"

She had to smile at his enthusiasm. "Well, I doubt that I will ever be famous. I'll be perfectly satisfied just to be the proprietress of a respectable millinery business. Do you really think I can do it?"

"I don't have a doubt in my mind! When we get to Apalachicola, I'll take you to the Mansion House Hotel and arrange for you to have a room until we find you a more permanent place."

"A hotel? Won't that be terribly expensive? I don't have—"

"Quit worrying about your finances, Margaret. This will all be considered an expense of our new business. This is not a gift, or even a loan. I consider it an investment in what is to become a very profitable new enterprise for both of us."

"Oh, Mikal. I just hope I won't disappoint you."

"I'm not concerned about that. Look, Margaret. We're coming up to the docks. There's the *Windsong* secured at the second mooring. Get ready to board. I'll have someone put your trunk in the storage area while I show you to your cabin."

❧

Margaret had almost forgotten how bouncy the sea could be. Lying on her bunk in the small cabin, she could see the big harvest moon through the porthole over her bed. Her stomach felt slightly queasy, and she wondered whether that feeling was brought on by the rolling motion of the boat or whether it was simply the result of so much excitement.

How long would Mikal stay in Apalachicola before he sailed away again? She would need his help to find someplace where she could work. Suppose he left her stranded there in that unfamiliar city with no one to call on for help. He had told her not to worry, but that was easier said than done. He was not the one who would be left on a strange street corner without enough money for even a loaf of bread. Oh, what was she getting herself into?

She ran her fingers over the smooth leather binding of her Bible and slipped it beneath her pillow. There was not enough light to read by, but it was comforting to know that she held God's words in her hands. And it was even more comforting to know that God held her, Margaret Porter, in the palms of His hands.

As the moon rose higher in the sky and was no longer visible through her small, round window, she lay in the darkness and whispered her prayer. "Dear Jesus, thank You for loving me when I know I don't deserve to be loved. And thank You for staying beside me and being my friend, because I surely am going to need a friend to help me get through the days ahead."

At last she lapsed into a dreamless sleep as the *Windsong* plowed steadily onward through the Gulf of Mexico, carrying Margaret closer and closer to her new home.

By morning, Margaret began to feel better. None of her troubles seemed quite as monumental in the light of day as they had in the still, dark night. Her stomach had quieted and she was beginning to feel hungry.

She slipped into the dress she had removed the night before and buttoned her high-top shoes. She remembered from her last journey where the dining room was located. Just a bowl of oatmeal and perhaps a piece of fruit would be nice.

She opened her cabin door and stepped out on the deck to greet the first day of the rest of her life.

eleven

For four days the *Windsong* bounced over the choppy, blue waters of the Gulf of Mexico. Margaret stood on the deck, holding to the railing to keep her balance, and strained her eyes for a sight of land. But all she had seen since leaving Tampa were the endless, white-capped waves that pounded the sides of the boat and sent a stinging spray of salt water across the decks.

She had only seen Mikal once or twice during the journey, and although she had met the seven other passengers, she still felt terribly alone.

A young man and his wife told her they had come from South Carolina to claim and settle on a piece of land in south Georgia. Their travels would take them up the Apalachicola River into an area reported to be abounding with fish and wild game. Hearing reports of the rich, red soil found there, they planned to establish a farm. They were an interesting couple, but they kept mostly to themselves. The other five passengers, all men, seemed preoccupied with the various business ventures on their minds, none of which held any interest for Margaret. Apparently they were all connected in some way to a group called the Apalachicola Land Company.

She was about to return to her cabin when she saw Mikal striding toward her across the deck, a smile widening his lips. "Enjoying your trip?" he asked her.

She wasn't sure how she should answer him. Enjoy? Did he think that for her this was simply a pleasure trip? "I—I'm finding everything satisfactory, thank you," she finally blurted. "How many more days will it take us to reach our port?"

He noted the dark circles growing beneath her eyes. "You're ready to plant your feet on dry soil, aren't you? We should see land by late this afternoon. We'll be dropping our anchor just off St. George Island."

"You mean we aren't going straight to Ap-Apalachicola?" She stumbled over the strange sounds of her new home. "What is on St. George Island?"

"Not very much, actually, except for the lighthouse." Mikal leaned against the rail and propped one foot on the lower bar. "Just a lot of sand dunes and old Indian mounds and, of course, pine trees and palmetto bushes. It's a great place to find unusual shells, though."

Margaret gave an exasperated sigh. She did not come on this tiresome journey to look for shells. "Then why would we bother to stop there at all?"

"St. George Island is just across the bay from Apalachicola. We'll have to wait there for a paddle wheeler to come and take us the rest of the way in. The *Windsong* draws too much water to cross Apalachicola Bay."

"Then will we get to the town by nightfall?" She looked up into his earnest blue eyes for her answer.

"We're going to try." He inched closer to her so that their arms touched, and Margaret felt that familiar tingle run up her spine, the sensation she kept trying to ignore.

"I–I suppose I should go to the cabin and prepare to diembark."

"What's to prepare? All you have to do is pick up your little valise and walk down the ramp. Are you trying to get rid of me?" He grinned, revealing his perfectly spaced, glistening white teeth. His eyes crinkled merrily at the corners as though he enjoyed some secret joke. Margaret had to resist an impulse to run her fingers over his smooth, sun-bronzed cheeks.

"Get rid of you? No, of course I'm not." She turned her eyes to the sea and tried to introduce a safer topic of conversation.

"When will you show me the supplies you brought from New York for my hats?"

"As soon as we find a place where you can set up a shop. I already have an idea about that, too, but there's someone I have to speak to about it before I can make you any promises."

"You know someone with a room I could use for my shop? Oh, tell me about it, please," she teased.

Mikal's brow creased as he tried to decide how much he should tell her before he checked with his friend John Gorrie. "I can't promise anything, Margaret, but last year a friend and I bought a building on Market Street. He was to sign up tenants for the stores while I've been away, but if one of them is still vacant, perhaps we might be able to set something up for you there."

"You own a building in Apalachicola?" The difficult word was beginning to roll more easily off of her tongue. "Would it be in a good location for my business?"

"I think it would be perfect. Market Street runs right through the heart of the business district. You'd be sure to gain a wide exposure. But if we find those units are already leased, we'll find you something else. Just keep the faith."

Faith! That word again. Whenever Mikal was beside her, she could almost believe in the things he told her, but whenever she was alone, she found them much harder to accept. But now, leaning against the deck rail with his arm touching hers, Margaret's tensions and loneliness melted away, and a feeling of peaceful contentment swept over her. Mikal always seemed to come up with a solution for every problem she encountered. Very soon now, if she could rely on his words, she would be starting her new life in an exciting coastal city, making and selling her hats and bonnets to the affluent society who lived there. And even though she knew that Mikal would be away much of the time traveling between New England and the gulf coast, at least their paths were sure to cross whenever he came to Apalachicola. After all, they were business partners now.

The wind ballooned her satin skirts, and the salt spray dotted them with moisture. Her hair tumbled about her face so that she continually pushed it from her eyes, and the deck rocked and swayed in a perpetual motion that made it difficult to maintain her balance. But in spite of all of this, she had a strong premonition that this special day would be forever etched in her memories as a turning point in her life.

~

When the *Windsong* dropped anchor off the shore of St. George Island, Margaret yearned to set her feet on firm, solid ground, but the captain had given orders to stay aboard until morning. They would spend the night on the ship in these inland waters calmed by the barrier island, and at first light, one of the paddle wheelers would come to transport them across the bay.

Margaret was disappointed. She had set her hopes on seeing the city where she had cast her fate. Another day's wait seemed an eternity, and the flickering lights across the bay only served to intensify her impatience. Couldn't they at least get out on St. George Island and walk around on land for a bit? She had posed the question to Mikal when he found her on deck, staring morosely across the bay as a rhythmic sweep of illumination danced across the water from the lighthouse tower.

"The mosquitoes would carry you away," he told her. "Besides, it might not be safe. The remote location of St. George Island makes it an ideal hideout for outlaws, runaway slaves, or even Indians."

That was enough to convince Margaret that she wanted to remain on the schooner. She doubted that outlaws would be interested in any of her meager possessions, and she was not afraid of poor runaway slaves, but Indians—well, now, that was another matter. The hair on the back of her neck raised just thinking about them.

She slapped at a mosquito who had chosen her arm for his supper. "Are the bugs always this bad?" she asked.

"Sometimes they're much worse," Mikal said. "Perhaps you should go below deck and try to get a good night's sleep. Tomorrow is sure to be a very busy day."

Margaret was so filled with excitement that she was not sure she could sleep at all, but she returned to her cabin and slipped out of her dress. She laid it across the end of her bed so that it would be ready for her when she woke up in the morning.

She listened to unfamiliar sounds echoing across the bay from the harbor: the blast of a steamboat whistle and shouts that floated across the water on the chill autumn air. Her bed swayed back and forth on the gentle ripples, rocking her until she drifted into unconsciousness. In her dream, she was surrounded by hundreds of unfinished hats, and angry customers were shouting and grabbing for them while she sat in a corner, frantically trying to complete them.

❧

"All aboard," the steamboat captain commanded. Margaret and the other passengers walked across the gangplank to board the three-decked paddle wheeler that would take them across Apalachicola Bay.

"Steady," Mikal said, taking hold of her elbow. "We don't want to have to jump in and pull anyone out of the water."

Margaret climbed the companionway that led to the upper deck in order to get the best possible view. She had never ridden on a paddle wheeler before, and she wanted to have every exciting moment stored in her memory. Standing against the rail of the upper deck, she could see the captain in the wheelhouse and the tall smokestacks that belched out great clouds of black smoke as the boat eased its way across the bay. And all the while, she could see the busy port of Apalachicola growing larger and larger before her eyes.

She grabbed the rail to keep from falling when the paddle wheeler touched the shore with a gentle jar. Crowds of people were milling around the docks to meet the incoming boats, people who were soon to be her neighbors.

I'm here at last, she thought. *I'm home!*

twelve

Mikal hailed a carriage and asked the driver to give him a hand with Margaret's trunk. He carried his own few belongings in a small canvas bag, and Margaret carried her valise. "To the Mansion House Hotel," Mikal told the driver.

"That sounds so grand, Mikal. I don't need anything fancy."

"It's the best place to stay when you come to Apalachicola. You've had a hard trip. You deserve to pamper yourself a little."

Margaret leaned forward for a better view of the busy Apalachicola streets. She found them fascinating, with no similarity at all to the quaint little village of Tampa. Activity buzzed all around her. As they rode away from the water-front and entered the residential areas, the horses' hooves clip-clopped along the wide brick streets, past homes that reminded Margaret of Savannah. She fought back the tears that sprang unbidden to her eyes. Her own home had been similar to many of the homes she passed along the oak-lined avenue.

The carriage stopped in front of a two-story brick edifice. The sign informed her that this was the Mansion House. "Stay here in the carriage until I make the arrangements," Mikal told her.

She slumped back against the plush burgundy upholstery. It felt so good not to be rocking and swaying! And it was good to sit back and let someone else do her planning for her. But this hotel looked terribly expensive, and in spite of Mikal's words of assurance, Margaret knew that she would have to look for more modest accommodations at once.

After several minutes, Mikal returned with a hotel attendant, and together they began to unload Margaret's trunk onto a small, wheeled carrier. The attendant rolled the trunk into the hotel, and Mikal helped Margaret down from the carriage. "Your trunk will be placed in your room. You'll be safe and comfortable here," he said. "Later I'll join you for supper in the dining room."

"You're leaving me now?"

He read a hint of panic in her question. "I thought you might want to rest after such a long journey. I have to go now to find my friend John Gorrie to find out if a portion of our building might still be available for your shop. Of course, if you'd like to come along, I'm sure John would be pleased to meet you."

"Oh, yes, I'd like that! Do you have time for me to freshen up a bit, or should I just come as I am?"

"I'm afraid I need to catch him as early in the day as possible. You see, in addition to being the city's postmaster, he's also a doctor, and he'll be out making his rounds before long. But you don't have to go with me. It's really up to you."

Margaret did not hesitate for a moment. She smoothed her hair, adjusted her redingote over her skirts and said, "I'm ready."

Mikal paid the driver and dismissed the carriage. "Dr. Gorrie's office is not far from here, and I think a walk on dry land will be good for both of us."

Margaret noticed as they walked along the street that people waved to Mikal and called his name. "You know a lot of people in this town, don't you?"

"Yes, I have a lot of friends here, but this place is growing and changing so fast, I couldn't possibly know them all. See that house over there? That's the Taylor house. Mr. Taylor is John's attorney, and mine too when I have need of one." They rounded the corner and crossed the street. "Here's where my friend has his medical practice, and he resides here, too."

Mikal led her up the flower-bordered walk and onto the porch of the two-story house. He raised the brass knocker and gave several sharp raps. The door was opened at once by a white-haired, uniformed Negro man. "Why, Mistah Mikal! Come right in. The doctor, he gonna be mighty glad to see you." Then, as his eyes fell on Margaret, he exclaimed, "Well, looka here! Who's this you brung along with you?"

"This is Miss Porter, a friend of mine, William. Has Dr. John been behaving himself while I've been away?"

The old man's white teeth sparkled against his dark skin, and he emitted a high, cackling laugh. "Hee-hee! I reckon as how you'd have to ask him about that, Mistah Mikal."

"Ask me what?" A short, portly gentleman wearing a long, white lab coat came striding down the hall. "Well, look who's back in town! And who's this charming lady you've brought with you?" John ushered them into his parlor. "Come in here where we can talk. William will bring us some tea."

Mikal began the introduction. "Margaret Porter, allow me to present Dr. John Gorrie, my good friend and business partner."

Margaret offered her hand and John clasped it so tightly that her fingers hurt, but she liked the man at once. His eyes met hers with a probing intensity, and his friendly smile made her feel as though she had known him for a long time. "Dr. Gorrie, I'm so glad to meet you. Mikal has told me many good things about you."

"Uh-oh! What kind of tales has Mikal been telling about me?" He winked at her and said, "You mustn't believe everything that sailor tells you! I'm likely not nearly as bad as he makes me out to be."

Laughter filled the room as William placed a tray of tea and petit fours on the table and began to fill the delicate porcelain cups.

"John," Mikal said in a more serious tone, "I know you

don't have time to socialize with us this morning, but I must ask you about our new building. Have you filled it with tenants yet?"

"Of the four units, three have been leased for a year and will soon be operating as respectable stores. The fourth, and I hope you won't be disappointed when I tell you this, but I turned down the man who tried to tie it up with a deposit."

"I'm not disappointed, John. In fact, I'm elated because, you see, I've come to think that I may have a use for one of the stores myself. But I'm more than a little curious as to why you refused to lease it to someone with ready cash."

"You won't be surprised when I tell you the man's name. Harry Robards!"

"Harry Robards wanted to lease our store? What does he want it for?" Mikal asked.

"I'm not really sure. Oh, he says he wants to open a little pipe and tobacco shop, but I have a feeling he may be using that as a front for some of his more, uh, questionable business enterprises."

Margaret's curiosity peaked, but her good manners did not allow her to ask any questions about Harry Robards.

"Anyway," John continued, "what did you have in mind for the store? Are you going to give up the life of a merchant seaman for that of a storekeeper?" He laughed at the incongruity of such an idea.

"Not for myself," Mikal explained. "For my business partner here." He indicated Margaret with a wave of his hand. "This lady has a real talent for turning out stylish hats and bonnets, and I've brought her the materials she will need to make them. All she needs now is a place to work."

John's eyes brightened. "A milliner? What an interesting idea. I don't believe we have ever had one in all of Apalachicola. By George, I think you might just have stumbled onto something there."

"John is always receptive to new ideas," Mikal explained to Margaret. "He has some very innovative ideas of his own which I'm sure he'll share with you when he has more time." Then turning back to John, he continued, "Our building should provide an excellent location for her shop, don't you think? And there's even a little room upstairs that she might be able to turn into living quarters."

Margaret jumped up from her chair, almost upsetting the teacup she held on her lap. "Oh, Mikal, it all sounds so perfect! When can I see it?"

"I'll give you the key," John said. "Why don't you take her right on over there, Mikal, because I have patients I must see. Just let me know what you decide, and you know I'll help any way I can."

The doctor reached under his white coat and extracted a large ring of keys from his trousers. Flipping through them, he settled on a long, silver skeleton key and removed it from the ring. "I think this is the one. I hope this works out to suit your purposes."

Margaret was so happy she could have hugged him. "Thank you for all your help, Dr. Gorrie!"

"The name is John. And you're very welcome, my dear. I'm glad to see that my friend Mikal has such good taste. Maybe he has more sense than I've been crediting him with." He gave Mikal a playful jab on the arm.

"I'll be in touch, John," Mikal said as he followed Margaret toward the front door. "Don't bother to see us out. We can take care of ourselves."

❧

Mikal slid the key into the lock and gave it a twist. He turned the knob and held the door open to allow Margaret to enter first. Trash and dust covered the oak plank floor, and Mikal was afraid that Margaret would be discouraged before she even got past the front door, but her eyes did not focus on the dirt and debris. Instead they circled the perimeter of the room and sparkled with excitement. "Oh, Mikal, this is going to be just perfect!" She moved across the floor, shuffling trash as she stepped gingerly across to the other side of the room. She ran her hand over one of the three long tables that constituted the room's only furniture. "This will make a perfect cutting table after I clean it up, and the other two tables could be used as counter space." Her excitement mounted. "If I could just get a few shelves put up, I'll take a broom and mop to this place and soon be ready to start making bonnets!"

"Let's see what the room upstairs is like," Mikal said, starting up the steps that rose from the back corner of the room. Margaret was quick to follow him.

The small attic room had three dirty windows that looked out onto Market Street, but the sloping ceiling made it impossible to stand up on the side of the room beside the windows.

Margaret hunched over and crept toward them. She ran a finger over the glass, leaving a streak in the dust. "As soon as I wash these windows, I'll make some gingham curtains to hang over them. I can just picture it all in my mind. It's going to be so pretty!"

Mikal could not picture this dismal little room becoming "pretty," even under Margaret's talented fingers, but he did not tell her so.

In one corner was a small, cast-iron cookstove. Against one wall, a single bed made from plain pine panels supported a thin mattress. A sawbuck table and a slat-backed rocker completed the meager furnishings. "Are you sure this place will be adequate for your needs, Margaret?"

"Oh, yes! When I get through with this place, you won't recognize it, Mikal. When can I begin?" Then she was hit with a thought that should have occurred to her before now. "Mikal, what is the rent for this place?"

"Look, Margaret. I thought we agreed that we were partners.

The rent will come from the profits as soon as there are some. Anyway, no one would rent this place the way it is now. Anything you do will only add to its value.

"Downstairs, I'd like to put in a few shelves along one wall to stock with merchandise other than hats," he continued. "That might give us an additional source of income."

"What kind of merchandise did you have in mind?" Margaret asked, leading the way back down the stairs. "Something else for the ladies, to go with their hats?"

"I've always thought I'd like to have a bookstore. We could just put in a few shelves of books to start and see how well they sell. I don't think we'd have so many customers that they'd interrupt your hat making too often. Do you think you could handle all of this by yourself?"

Margaret gave the matter a few moments of serious thought. She did hate interruptions when she was cutting out her bonnets, but if she were to run a millinery store, she would probably have to do her cutting and sewing after hours anyway. She'd have to put the customers' needs first, no matter what she sold. "I'm sure I could handle the sale of books alongside my bonnets," she said. "What kind of books would we sell?"

"Useful books. Bibles, of course, and dictionaries, and reference books. And some just for reading pleasure, like *The Last of the Mohicans*. I don't have a lot of time for reading, but I sure enjoyed that! I'd bring the books down from New York, and I could bring some magazines that show the latest fashions for women. I think the women of Apalachicola would snap them up in a hurry, and they might even give you some ideas for your hats."

"Could I start today?" Margaret pleaded. "I'd like to get the little room upstairs cleaned so that I could move over here from the hotel."

Mikal knew that her main concern was her lack of money,

but he could see that she needed to get some rest. She had some hard work ahead of her. "Margaret, I want to take you back to the hotel now. You can have a nice, relaxing bath and rest for a few hours. I'll come back to have supper with you, as I promised earlier, and then you need to get a good night's sleep. Tomorrow will be soon enough to start on this job."

"I suppose you're right," Margaret agreed reluctantly. "But I want to start early in the morning, if it's all right with you."

"I'll bring in some cleaning supplies, and I'll see about getting enough lumber to put up some shelves. I'll put in a few shelves upstairs, too. I can work with you all day tomorrow and the next day, but after that, I'm afraid you'll be on your own for a while. Those Georgia and Alabama cotton farmers are beginning to come in with their bales of cotton. As soon as the schooner is loaded, I'll be heading back to New York."

Margaret tried not to show her disappointment. Mikal was so good to her, the best friend she had ever had. She couldn't expect him to drop everything to take care of her needs. She would have to learn to depend on herself. "Mikal, you still haven't shown me the millinery supplies you brought from New York. When do I get to see them?"

Mikal led her outside to the sidewalk and turned back to lock the door. "The boxes are still on the *Windsong*. I'll have them brought to the store as soon as we get the place cleaned up a bit. You wouldn't want to get dust and grime on your new fabrics, would you?"

Of course, Margaret agreed that she would not. Still, she found it hard to be patient when she was so anxious to see the materials she would soon be transforming into stylish bonnets and hats.

"I'm going to have a sign made," Mikal announced as they began their walk toward the Mansion House. "I can see it now: *Margaret's Millinery Shoppe.*"

Margaret could see it, too, and it caused her heart to pound with excitement. "But what about your books? Shouldn't the sign say something about them, too?"

"This town has a way of passing news around. I think word will spread fast enough once we have our shelves stocked."

The two business partners walked hand in hand, each wondering just how far this new partnership was destined to extend.

thirteen

Margaret rolled up the sleeves of her calico dress and set to work with the new broom that Mikal had brought. Together they had carted out three bushel baskets of trash this morning, and they had not even started on the upstairs yet. She wiped her face with the edge of her muslin apron. My, it was hot for a November day!

Margaret coughed and choked as dust raised by her broom spiraled around her. One thing was certain: if she ever got this place clean, it would never again collect this much dust and filth, at least not as long as *she* had anything to do with it!

On hands and knees, she and Mikal worked side by side all morning, using stiff scrub brushes, lye soap, and buckets of cold water that Mikal carried in from the backyard pump. Even though perspiration ran down her cheeks, working alongside Mikal gave Margaret a happy, secure feeling. The hours seemed to fly, and by noon, they were ready to tackle the room upstairs.

Mikal stood in the center of the spotless wooden floor and admired the fruit of their morning's efforts. "I'd never have believed it possible! Say, there's a café on the corner where we can get a bite to eat. Do you like fresh oysters?"

"Love 'em! I've only had them once or twice, but my father was very fond of seafood, particularly shellfish. Whenever he could buy it fresh from the ocean, he always brought some home."

"Apalachicola probably has the most and the best oysters found anywhere in the world. At least, that's what people around here say. Let's go try some and make up our own minds!"

The café was bustling with business. Mikal and Margaret sat across from each other at a small table near the window, and Margaret found that oysters were every bit as good as she remembered them, perhaps even better. Certainly they were much larger than the ones she had eaten in Savannah. She could not dispute the extravagant claim of the locals. She and Mikal ate them on crackers and washed them down with hot coffee laced with thick, sweet cream.

"I can't remember when I've enjoyed a meal so much," Margaret said, wiping her lips on her napkin. But her thoughts were still focused on the new store with her own little room above. "Mikal, I don't want to rush you through your meal, but do you think we could get the upstairs done before dark and have my trunk brought over from the hotel? I'd really like to move in as soon as possible."

Mikal was as anxious as Margaret to get the work finished, but for a different reason. He would be leaving Apalachicola in two more days, and he wanted to make sure that all the heavy work was taken care of before he left. But he did think that Margaret deserved a few days of luxury before she began work in her millinery shop. Life was not going to be easy for her once she settled into her room on Market Street.

"We can get the work done, but why don't you enjoy a few days in the hotel before you have your trunk sent over? You can have warm baths and a comfortable bed to sleep in. Do you realize that after you move, all your water will have to be carried up the steps from the pump in the backyard? And the wood for your stove will have to be carried up, too."

"I—I can manage." Margaret tried to project more assurance in her words than she actually felt. She had never before been responsible for carrying in her own wood and water. But she was fast learning to do a lot of things she had never done before. Why, until this morning, she had never even scrubbed a floor!

"We'd better get back to work, then," Mikal said. "If you're bound and determined to stay in that room tonight, we have a lot to do between now and dark!"

❧

John Gorrie invited them both for supper on the night before Mikal's departure. After starting the meal with fresh conch chowder, William served them fresh pork roast, baked sweet potatoes topped with hand-churned butter, tender young pods of okra from the garden, and a basket of beaten biscuits made from his own secret recipe.

Margaret groaned when she heard him announce dessert, but the compote of fresh tropical fruits was the perfect ending for the delicious meal.

"Let's take our demitasse in the parlor," John suggested. "And then I have something I'd like to show you."

As they moved into the parlor, Mikal explained to Margaret that John was an innovator and an inventor, and he almost always had something interesting to share. "What is it this time, John?"

As they sat sipping their coffee, John told them of his latest idea. "I've lost several patients to high fever, and I've tried various ways to lower their body temperatures. Cool compresses help to a degree, but I think I'm about to come up with a way to cool their entire room."

"And do you think that would lower their body temperature?" Margaret asked.

"I'm almost certain it would. I don't have the machine perfected yet, but as soon as I do, I plan to apply for a patent on it. This could be quite a revolutionary development in combating some of these virulent fevers we continue to encounter down here in the tropics."

"That sounds exciting, John," Mikal said. "Of course, I hope you never have to use it on me, but if you should. . ."

"Enough about me," John interrupted. "Tell me what you

two have accomplished since I last saw you."

Margaret drained the last drops of coffee from the tiny cup and placed it on the tray. "John, I want you to come by and see for yourself. Mikal brought me the most gorgeous fabrics from New York that I have ever seen!" Her face glowed with animation. "And the trims! There are ribbons and laces and flowers, and he even brought feathers. I'm going to have the most stunning hats and bonnets you've ever laid your eyes on! I do hope you'll stop in to see."

"I shall," John promised. "Mikal has already asked me to keep an eye on you while he's away, to make sure that you have everything you need. If you think of anything else that you need, just send a message to my address, and I'll see that you're taken care of properly."

"He really means that, Margaret. Don't feel reluctant to call on him," Mikal assured her.

"Thank you. You're both so very kind to me."

John cleared his throat. "Well, if everyone is finished with the coffee, let's move upstairs where you can see my new cooling machine. I'll turn it on for you and show you how it works."

❧

Margaret did not go to the docks to see the paddle wheeler that would carry Mikal and his cargo out to St. George Island to board the *Windsong*. She had come to depend on Mikal, but more than that, she was forced to admit that she had grown to love him. She told herself that if she kept busy enough, hard work would keep her from missing Mikal while he was away, but it did not work out that way. At night she dreamed of him, and by day he invaded her thoughts no matter what she was doing.

Mikal had never spoken to her of love. She realized that he thought of her only as a good friend, and as such, he went out of his way to help her, just as he did with his other friends.

That was just part of his nature. Even the one kiss he had placed on her lips had not been a lover's kiss. Margaret was certain that he would never offer her real love, because Mikal was in love with the sea.

For the first few days, she was able to work with few interruptions, because word of her shop had not yet spread about the town. This was just as well, she thought, because it gave her enough of a head start to finish a few hats and bonnets for the shelves and have something to show her customers when they began to arrive.

Her first customers were two very stylish young matrons who introduced themselves as Harriet Raney and Mary Elizabeth Messina. They were both looking for hats in specific colors to wear when the opera house opened next week.

"Not red and not pink. Something about the color of a raspberry," Mrs. Raney specified. "Can you show me something like that?"

"I don't have anything like that today, ma'am, but if you can give me a day or two, I think I can come up with just what you want."

"Well, I want something, too," her friend said. "Mine must be green—a dark, emerald green with a pale green lining. Don't you think that would be pretty?"

"I made one like that for a lady in Fort Brooke a short while ago," Margaret told her. "I added a little sprig of violets just over the right ear, and she was very happy with the effect."

"Oh, yes," Mrs. Messina said, clasping her hands together in delight. "I hadn't thought of violets, but that would be grand."

"Well, what are you going to put on mine to make it special, too?" Harriet Raney asked, obviously anxious to keep pace with her friend.

Margaret gave the matter some thought before she answered. "How about a pleated band of black velvet across the crown and black velvet ribbon ties. I saw one similar to that in one of Godey's fashion plates."

"Yes, yes! How soon could you have mine ready?"

"I can have them both done by the end of the week," Margaret promised. She would have to work late by candlelight in order to finish them in time, but these were her first customers, and she wanted to make sure they were well satisfied. Whatever their reactions, they were sure to tell their friends.

They agreed on a price, and the two ladies left the store with smiles on their faces. Margaret was pleased, too! Her first sale!

She was bent over a box, getting the fabric and notions she would need for her first two orders when she heard the front door open and footsteps approach her counter. She straightened up and turned to see her next customer and was surprised to see that it was not a lady as she had expected, but a gentleman.

Margaret caught her breath! He looked as though he had just stepped off one of the fashion plates in her newest copy of *Lady's Book*. Instead of being dressed in the usual clothes of the working class, he wore a blue velvet waistcoat over a shirt that was frilled not only down the front but over his wrists. He carried a gold-tipped cane, and he removed his tall black hat as he walked toward her. "Good morning, madam," he said, sweeping a low bow.

He was very tall, and his neatly trimmed mustache matched the color of his sleek, black hair. His handsome and stylish appearance was startling, but Margaret saw something in his eyes that made her slightly uneasy. "May I help you, sir?"

"I was just roaming through the neighborhood and thought I would drop in to welcome you to our town. Are you finding our local hospitality acceptable?" He continued to smile, but his expression seemed to reflect a private joke he was not yet ready to share with her. His dark, piercing eyes perused the store.

"Why yes, I—everyone has been very nice to me, thank you. I don't suppose I could interest you in a bonnet." She was trying to subtly indicate that he had probably stumbled into her shop by mistake.

"Well, now, you just might. Let me see what you have."

His smile, which was very akin to a smirk, warned Margaret that he was not a serious customer, yet she could not offend him by turning him away. "Most of my hats are custom-made, sir. If you would give me some idea of the lady who might be wearing the hat, perhaps I could possibly make some suggestions. May I inquire your name?"

"Of course." He held out his hand. "I'm Harry Robards. And you. . .?"

Harry Robards! The man to whom John refused to lease this store! What had John said about his questionable business enterprises? Margaret swallowed the lump that felt like an egg in her throat, and without offering her hand, she stammered, "I–I'm Mar—uh, Miss Porter, the proprietress."

Harry dropped his hand to his side. "I'm pleased to make your acquaintance, Mar-uh-Miss Porter," he mimicked, and Margaret felt the blood rush to her face. "Well, I can see that I have disturbed your work, so I will leave now, but I'll be back another day. You can count on it, Miss Porter." Harry turned on his heels and walked toward the door. With his hand on the knob, he turned back. "Perhaps one evening you would do me the honor of dining with me."

Without waiting for her reply, he turned and walked out the door.

fourteen

By her third week in her new home, news of Margaret's millinery shop had spread like wildfire, and she was having trouble keeping up with the demand. With Christmas just around the corner, it seemed that every lady in Apalachicola wanted a new hat to wear during the holidays. Now she was only taking orders that could be filled in January, and she even had several commitments for Easter. If things kept up at this rate, she would soon have to hire help with the cutting and basting, saving only the finishing for her own skilled fingers.

Fortunately, she had secured the daily services of a local ten-year-old schoolboy. Alex came by early each morning to fill her wood box and water buckets. After school, he stopped by again to empty her slops and run errands about town. He was happy for the few coins she gave him, and relief from these simple tasks allowed Margaret more hours to devote to her millinery work.

John Gorrie had dropped in once to see her store, and he was extremely complimentary of what she had accomplished. Then he extended an invitation. "I attend Sunday services at the church on the corner near my house," he told her. "If you would care to join me, I will send a carriage for you."

Margaret worked hard in her shop all week, with little time to think of outside activities. Even the leather Testament that Mikal had given her was beginning to gather dust on the shelf in her upstairs room. Although she appreciated the doctor's kind gesture, she had no intention of giving up her one free day to sit through church services. "Thank you, John, but I–I already have plans."

When Sunday dawned bright and clear, Margaret's only plans were to sleep late and spend leisurely hours looking through her fashion magazines. But as sunlight streamed through her bedroom windows, she realized that she had hardly set foot out of doors all week.

One of her customers had mentioned a grove of walnuts near the creek that ran behind her house. *How nice it would be to have a basket of nuts to roast for the holidays, especially if Mikal is back in town!*

The simple cotton dresses she had scorned when she first arrived in Tampa were now the most practical and comfortable clothes in her wardrobe. If she should have a slow-down of business, she would like to stitch another calico frock or two for her daily use.

Today she chose the brown gingham, and noticed that the bottom of the hem was beginning to fray. Perhaps she could stitch a bias binding around the bottom to extend its life. She covered her dress with her muslin pinafore apron and chose a wide-brimmed calico bonnet to shield her face from the sun.

Margaret felt lighthearted as she walked out the door. This was the first time since her arrival in Apalachicola that she had decided to forget about work and do something simply for fun. With a basket over her arm, she set off in the direction of the creek.

When she reached the edge of the creek, she turned north according to the directions she had been given and walked alongside the stream that would eventually empty into the Apalachicola River. She walked for almost a mile, but still she had not seen the first sign of a walnut tree. She hadn't realized it would be so far. As she walked along the creek bank, palmettos pricked at her ankles, and the surrounding woods grew dense and dark, but still there were no walnut trees. If she did not find them soon, she would be forced to turn back. But not because she was afraid. After all, there was no way she could become lost as long as she followed the stream, and it was really quite pleasant out here alone with only the birds to keep her company.

She heard sounds of rushing water, and she observed that the creek had now grown wider and deeper with whirlpools and falls. As she continued on, Margaret moved away from the edge to make sure she did not slip into the water that seemed to grow more turbulent by the minute. And then she saw the walnut trees just ahead.

The trees were much too tall for Margaret to reach up into their branches, but there were plenty of nuts scattered all over the ground. She scooped them up with her free hand and soon had her basket almost full. What fun! She could still hear the rushing water that would lead her home as soon as her basket was filled. What a wonderful decision she had made to come here today!

But her happiness turned to apprehension when she heard a noise through the trees. It sounded as though an animal was approaching. Likely, it was just a harmless fox. But to be on the safe side, Margaret took her basket and eased her way back toward the creek, careful to make no unnecessary noise. When she reached the creek, she turned back to make sure that the animal had not followed her, and her apprehension changed to sheer panic!

Beneath the walnut trees, an Indian sat tall and erect on his large, white horse, holding his bow and arrow and looking straight at Margaret! Her heart pounded and cold perspiration broke out across her forehead. Her whole body began to tremble. What should she do? She could never outrun this red-skinned savage, but neither could she just stand here and wait for him to come and claim her scalp! She felt detached from the sound of her own piercing scream that filled the air before she broke out into a run along the creek bank. Just as she reached the point where she had seen the falls, her footing slipped and she catapulted down the bank and into the deep, roiling water. Her basket flew into the air and walnuts scattered around her like hail. Her scream continued until her mouth filled with water. She bobbed up once, choking and thrashing, and caught a glimpse of the Indian looking down at her from the steep bank. Which would be worse, to drown in the creek or be brutally murdered as Allen Fairchild had been? She did not have time to think about it before she fainted and sank again beneath the rushing water.

Margaret had given herself over to the water when she became conscious of strong arms beneath her, lifting her from the water and carrying her up the steep embankment. She opened her eyes just long enough to glimpse the color of the arms that carried her—a coppery red—before she fainted again.

❧

As Margaret slid back into consciousness and her world began to come into focus again, she remembered everything that had happened to her. She was afraid to fully open her eyes lest she should see a whole tribe of Indians surrounding her. The only sound that she could hear was the nearby rushing water. At last, she opened her eyes and scanned her surroundings and was amazed to discover that she was *alone!* Was that Indian watching from the shelter of the woods, just waiting for her to make a move? She tried to get up, but her limbs felt weak and useless. When she finally managed to pull herself to a sitting position, she found that someone had made a soft pile of leaves for her bed. A brightly woven blanket covered her wet clothes and shielded her body from the chilly December breeze. And to compound her confusion, her basket sat beside her, filled with walnuts—even more than she had gathered to start with.

Dazed, she stood on shaky legs. She could make no sense

from any of this, but she wanted to distance herself from this place as fast as she could. She folded the blanket and left it beneath the trees. Then, slipping her basket over her arm, she began the long walk home.

By the time she reached her shop, the sun had dropped low in the sky. Her legs ached and her teeth chattered from cold. Wet clothes clung to her body, and her hair was plastered to her neck and face. Her hands were shaking so that she had trouble fumbling with the key, but finally she opened the door and made her way up the stairs.

Placing the basket of walnuts on the table, she stripped off her clothes and left them in a wet heap on the floor. How she longed for a soak in a nice, warm tub, but the best she could do was a quick splash with cold water from her pitcher and washbowl. She donned her dry chemise and sank onto her thin, hard mattress. Later she would try to make sense of what had happened to her today. Right now, she just wanted to put it all out of her mind.

She pulled a blanket around her shoulders, but still she could not quell the shaking of her body. A fire in her cook-stove would be nice, but she lacked the energy to get up and start one.

For the first time in her life, she had come face to face with a real Indian. She had not expected to live to tell about it. In her helpless condition, the man could have killed her or kidnapped her for terrible purposes, but instead he had saved her life. He had even gathered her spilled walnuts and tried to make her comfortable.

What was it Mikal had told her? Something about not condemning a whole race because of the actions of a few. *There are good Indians and bad, just as there are good and bad white men.* She could almost hear Mikal's voice repeating the words for which she had chastised him so severely.

Oh, Mikal, I need you so! She had never felt so alone. Her eyes fell on the Testament gathering dust on the shelf beside her bed. For the first time in weeks, she lifted it and opened to Matthew. Running her finger down the page, she found a verse she remembered: "Lo, I am with you alway, even unto the end of the world."

In the fading light of day, the tension began to gradually seep from her body. She was not alone! Christ was with her and would always be, even unto the end of the world! As a sense of peace enveloped her, Margaret closed her eyes and slept.

☙

Monday was such a busy day that Margaret did not have time to think about the strange events of the day before. She was bent over her cutting table, slicing her scissors into a piece of plush red velvet, when she heard someone enter her door. She laid down her work and turned to greet her customer. "Good morning. May I help you?"

Oddly, instead of one of her familiar ladies, this client was a well-dressed gentleman. "How may I help you, sir?"

"I would like to place an order for a lady's bonnet. I believe that black velvet would be the best choice of material. It needs to be—well, this bonnet is for a very special lady, and it should be made of the very finest fabric in your stock."

Assuming that he wanted a special gift for his wife or sweetheart, Margaret nodded. "I understand. Let me show you some designs." She reached for one of her magazines.

"The lady wishes the bonnet to be conservative yet elegant," he said.

Margaret lifted her eyebrows. "Oh, then this is not to be a surprise?"

"Oh, no. In fact, it is she who has heard of your excellent reputation, and she has decided that she would like to have one of your creations."

Margaret slid the magazine back into place. "If this is not

to be a surprise, sir, then I'd like to suggest that you bring the lady in so that we can take measurements and be assured of a perfect fit. I can show her what materials I have and offer her some choices in the style."

"Quite impossible," the gentleman stated emphatically. "Well, I may as well tell you," he said, looking around the shop to make sure there was no one else who could overhear his words. He dropped his voice to a whisper. "The lady is the diva who is scheduled to appear at the opera house next month."

Margaret gasped. "And she wants *me* to make her a bonnet?"

"Yes. So you see why bringing her here is not possible. She rarely goes out in public, where people besiege her for autographs. Why, some of them get so excited that they literally rip her garments to obtain a souvenir. I will leave it to your good judgment as to the style of the bonnet, and of course you will be generously compensated for your work. When can I expect to pick it up?"

"I. . .you. . .I'll have it ready for you in a week," Margaret stammered. She would stay up nights if she had to in order to finish the order in time. When word of this got around town, Margaret was sure to be deluged with work.

Just imagine! I, Margaret Porter, will be making a bonnet for the famous diva of the opera!

fifteen

On a cold afternoon in January, Mikal walked unannounced into Margaret's Millinery Shoppe with an armload of boxes. He dropped them on the counter and said, "Happy New Year! I'm back!"

When she saw him, Margaret squealed with delight and ran around the counter, where he stood with his arms outstretched. "Mikal!"

He lifted her like a rag doll, twirling her around and around. When he finally let her feet touch the floor, she was so dizzy that she fell against him and lingered a moment longer than necessary when she felt the warmth of his strong embrace. "Oh, Mikal, I'm so glad you're back. I've so much to tell you!"

"And I have things to tell you, too." Pointing to the boxes on the counter, he said, "These are some of the books I brought from New England to stock our shelves, and there's more to be brought in from the *Windsong* later today. They'll be delivered by one of the deckhands."

Her cheeks were flushed with excitement. "I hope you've brought more fabrics, too. I'm running low on several things, and I'm completely out of red velvet. The holidays, you know."

He let his eyes roam over the store. "I can see you've been busy. You've done wonders here, Margaret."

Their conversation was cut short by three customers who came in together, each wanting to place an order for Easter.

"I'll get out of your way," Mikal offered. "You take care of your customers while I open these boxes and begin to put the books on the shelves."

"Books?" one of the ladies asked. "What kind of books do you have?"

"Why, we have several kinds, ma'am. I'll have some of them unpacked by the time you place your orders with Miss Porter, and you'll be welcome to look them over."

"You mean they're for sale?" another of the ladies asked.

"Yes, ma'am. Miss Porter will soon be selling books as well as bonnets." He smiled politely before he turned his back to them and began to open his boxes.

"My, isn't our city becoming progressive?" the customer remarked. "Just think, 1837 has barely begun, and already we're getting a new bookstore! We don't have to send all the way to New Orleans for the latest millinery fashions anymore, and soon we'll be able to buy all the newest books and magazines, too. It's so exciting to be living in this modern age!"

Mikal smiled to himself as the ladies behind him continued to expound on the wonders of the modern world. He could not disagree that these were indeed exciting times. He and Margaret were standing on the threshold of opportunity. If only he felt as confident about his personal life as he did about his business, he would be the happiest man on earth.

He had wrestled with decisions all the way from New York to Apalachicola, and still he did not know what he should do about Margaret. He had grown to love her more than he had ever thought it possible to love any living creature, but because he loved her so much, he would not risk hurting her by declaring it. He knew that for him, marriage was out of the question, and he wanted desperately to be fair to Margaret. He also knew that she was attracted to him, for whatever reason. Perhaps he should discourage this friendship that threatened to develop into something more. Margaret was a young and attractive woman. She needed a chance to broaden her acquaintances to include men who were eligible for a lasting relationship that Mikal could never offer.

He had asked God to lead him in the paths he should follow, but those paths had not yet been revealed to him. He would continue to pray, and he would seek John Gorrie's advice when the opportunity presented itself. John was the smartest and most sensible man he knew, and even more important, John was a dedicated Christian. This would not be the first matter on which Mikal had sought his advice.

Between customers, Mikal asked Margaret, "What time do you close the shop?"

"Six o'clock," she told him. "But that's when my real work here begins. I do most of my cutting and sewing at night now, because that's the only free time I have."

"Well, you must make an exception tonight. At six o'clock, we're locking up, and we're going to the dining room of the Mansion House. After we enjoy a good meal, we'll sit in the lobby and talk. We have a lot of things to catch up on, so we might as well find a comfortable place where we won't be interrupted."

Margaret did not even have time to answer him before the next customer walked in. "Good afternoon, miss. May I help you?"

ら

For dining in the Mansion House Hotel, Margaret wore her green satin gown. With its puffy leg-o'-mutton sleeves, it was the more elegant of the only two dressy outfits she had left. She longed for some of the trousseau gowns that she cut up to make bonnets for the ladies from Fort Brooke, but there was no need to look back on that now. They had served a good purpose when she had needed them most.

Across the table, Mikal appeared very debonair in his closely fitted waistcoat. His dark blue eyes sparkled in the flickering candlelight. Margaret's heart was so full of love for him that she could hardly swallow. But she valued his friendship too much to risk spoiling it by letting him know of her feelings. She tried to nibble at her food and carry on a sensible conversation.

"I have missed you, Margaret."

"And I you, Mikal." Trying to maintain a steady voice, she moved to a less personal subject. "How was the trip this time? Was the weather pleasant?"

"It was pleasant enough."

Margaret thought that Mikal seemed moody tonight, not at all like his usual lighthearted self. Was he disappointed in the way she was handling the business, or did he have something else on his mind?

The first course, a delicate clam chowder, was served in thin, porcelain cups. Margaret's stomach felt just as it had when she rode the high seas, but tonight her nerves and not ocean waves were the cause.

"How long will you be able to stay in Apalachicola this time?" she asked. If the past was any indication, he would be sailing away in just a few short days.

"I'm not sure; it'll depend on what we can contract to haul north on the *Windsong*. There's a lot of cotton coming in at this time of the year, and I'm working on an arrangement to fill the schooner on the return trips from New York. I need to talk to John tomorrow. He's asked me to help him on a very big project."

"Something to do with his cooling machine?"

"Not this time. This has to do with his church. He has an idea of putting up a very large and elaborate structure for Trinity. He has his heart set on something he saw in New York, a Greek Revival church. The trouble is, he'd have to get most of the work done in New York and then have it shipped here by schooner. I'm not even sure that's possible, but if he's able to bring his plans to fruition, Apalachicola will have a church like no other in the South."

"You'd bring a whole church down on the *Windsong?*

Could you do that?"

"It would have to be shipped in pieces. Right now we're just in the talking stage, but if he can pull together the finances, I'd sure like to give it a try. It would work in well with the cotton trade, because I never have trouble filling my cargo going north. If this thing works out, he'd pretty much tie up the space for a while on return trips."

Margaret's face clouded. "Then you wouldn't be able to bring down millinery supplies or books?"

Mikal laughed and reached across the table to cover her hand. "Margaret, don't worry your pretty head about that. You just keep making your bonnets, and I'll make sure that you don't run out of supplies. As for the books, we'll see how these first ones move before I bring in any more."

The feel of his warm hand covering hers sent tingles up Margaret's arm that coursed through her whole body. She willed her trembling hand not to betray her emotions. "I've sold two books already, Mikal. As soon as word gets around, I'm sure we'll need more." She slid her hand from under his. "We'd better eat our soup before it gets cold."

After a deliciously satisfying meal, Margaret led the way into the plush hotel lobby. Mikal, following close behind, resisted the urge to hold her hand. He wanted a clear head when he talked to her tonight.

She sat on the sofa and saved room for him beside her, but he chose a chair that faced her.

Just one more indication that his feelings for me are based on nothing more than friendship, Margaret thought, adjusting her green skirts over the couch.

"Margaret," he began, "it concerns me that you are spending all your time in the shop. I know that your work is very demanding, but I'd like you to find time to get out and meet people, socialize more."

Margaret's lips curved in a smile. "And where would you

like for me to do this socializing? In the tavern down the street?"

"You know me better than that. I just thought perhaps you might get involved with a church group. You could meet nice people and get out and have some fun once in a while." He did not add that she might also have the spiritual awakening he continued to pray for.

"I'll give the matter some thought," she promised. "How about you? Are you finding time to 'socialize,' as you put it?" She could not help but wonder if someone in New York watched for his return there with the same eagerness that she waited for him here.

"It's different for me. The sea is my life, Margaret." He looked deep into her eyes and spoke those words with a severity that frightened her. What was he trying to tell her?

"I do get out of the store sometimes on Sundays," she said, wanting to shift the conversation to safer ground. "In fact, I had quite an adventure on Sunday before last. Let me tell you about that."

Margaret began to tell him of her trip to the walnut grove and her fall into the creek. Then she told him about the Indian who had come to her rescue. She did not fill in all the details of how her terrified flight had caused her to fall or of the ups and downs of her emotions that followed. She simply ended her story by saying that she could not swim, and the man had pulled her from the current and carried her safely to dry land. "So you see, I don't spend all of my time in the shop!"

Mikal's heart stood still as he listened to her story. "Margaret, you should not have wandered off into the woods alone. It's much too dangerous. Renegade Indians and outlaws roam freely through the territory. Things here are not as they are in the States, where you have laws and people to enforce them. Please promise me that you won't do anything like that again."

Having been scared out of her wits that frightening Sunday

afternoon, Margaret had long since resolved not to repeat her adventure, but what right did Mikal have to tell her what she could and could not do? If he were so concerned about her welfare, why didn't he stay around and take care of her?

"I'm well able to take care of myself, Mikal. Please don't concern yourself about my safety."

"Listen to me, Margaret. . ."

"It's getting late, Mikal. I think we should start walking back now. I open my shop at eight in the morning, and it's already half past nine."

Without further words, Mikal rose and escorted her out the door to the street. When he tried to hail a hackney, she stopped him. "It's so pleasant out tonight. Let's just walk."

They walked along the street in silence, each engrossed in serious thoughts, but they did not hold hands, although a lover's moon beamed down on them from the starry night sky.

sixteen

Margaret was up at first light, using her morning cup of tea to wash down a piece of stale cornbread. She smoothed her blanket over her mattress and dressed in her work clothes. She had several bonnets to trim before her shop opened at eight.

Downstairs at her cutting table, she worked furiously, letting her scraps of thread and cloth fall on the floor beside her. Alex would soon be in to sweep up before he went to school. How fortunate she was to have found such a dependable lad!

When she heard a rap on her front door, she assumed that it would be Alex, and she rose to let him in.

"Good morning, Margaret! I hope I'm not interrupting your work." Mikal stepped into the shop with another box of books. "I'll try not to disturb you. This is my last box of books to shelve, and I wanted to get on with it early, because this is the last you'll see of me for a while."

Margaret's heart skipped a beat, and her breath caught in her throat. "Surely you're not leaving town so soon!"

"No, nothing like that. But I told you about John Gorrie's idea for the new building for his church. He and I will be in meetings most of today with some of the local bankers, discussing the financial feasibility. Then for the next few days we'll be looking over his plans to see what all might be involved in shipping such a large structure. He has the idea of getting most of the actual construction done in New York and then having the church building shipped to Apalachicola in four different sections."

"I've never heard of such a thing! Is this sort of thing done often?"

Mikal chuckled. "I have to admit this is a first for me, and frankly, we aren't sure whether the idea will work or not. That's what we're going to spend the next several days trying to decide. I hope—"

His sentence was severed when the front door swung open and Alex dashed in waving a piece of paper in his hand. "Miss Margaret, here's—"

"Alex, say good morning to Mr. Lee. He's part owner of this shop, and I've already told him what a help you've been for me."

Alex murmured a hasty "pleased to meetcha" before he turned back to Margaret. "I'm supposed to give you this note. Mr. Robards gave me a whole dollar to deliver it."

"A *dollar*," Margaret said, amazed at the amount quoted for a simple delivery. "It must be a very important message!"

"Yes'm, an' he told me to wait for your answer, an' if I bring it back to him, he's gonna gimme some more money! So could you please, ma'am, go ahead an' read it an' send me back with your answer? I'll hurry up an' come back here to do my chores."

Margaret stepped over to the counter to read her note, but Mikal was right beside her. "Robards? That wouldn't be Harry Robards, would it?"

Margaret did not answer, but held the message close to her chest as she read so as not to reveal its contents. "Miss Porter, I am humbly requesting the pleasure of your company for dinner this evening at seven. I hope that you will honor my request, as I have some matters of great importance to discuss with you. Your faithful servant, Harry Robards."

Alex stood impatiently shifting from one foot to the other with obvious visions of wealth dancing in his young head. "So what kin I tell him, Miss Margaret? He said if you tell him you'll go, he'll give me another dollar, but if you say no, then I only get fifty cents."

Mikal's face was crimson with rage. "Tell him the lady is not interested," he said to Alex. "You tell him that, and I'll give you the dollar myself!"

But as Alex turned to go, Margaret grabbed him by the sleeve. "Just a minute, Alex. That message was sent to me, and I believe that I'm the one from whom Mr. Robards is expecting a reply." *How dare Mikal try to make decisions for me! He's going to spend the next three days running around town without allotting so much as an hour of his time with me, and he thinks I'll just sit here waiting for his return? Well, he's got another think coming.* "Alex, tell Mr. Robards that I will be expecting him at seven."

"Yes'm." The confused child went running out of the store, eager to deliver his message and collect his money from someone—anyone!

"I'll be back in a minute to do my chores," he called over his shoulder.

Margaret turned fiery eyes to Mikal. "When it comes to the business, I don't mind your suggestions, Mikal, but when it comes to my personal life, that should be none of your concern."

"Margaret, do you even know who Harry Robards is?" Mikal raked his fingers through his blond hair in frustration. "Have you ever heard of Lewis Robards?" He saw by her expression that she did not recognize the name. "He's the scoundrel who was married to Rachel Jackson. He treated her shamefully and told her that he had obtained a divorce decree nullifying their marriage. She married Andrew Jackson, only to find out later that her divorce was not legal. That poor woman lived in shame and embarrassment until Andy took all the steps to put things right. Why, I hear tell the poor lady was so embarrassed that, up until the day she died, she hardly set foot outside her own door."

As shocking as these facts were, Margaret was determined not to give in to Mikal's possessive manner. "Well, I don't see what Lewis's actions have to do with Harry. I suppose you are telling me that they are related, but surely Harry can't be held responsible for something Lewis has done. Why, Mikal, you're the very one who told me not to be prejudiced against one for the actions of another. Don't you remember?"

Mikal struggled to control his temper. It was not Margaret who caused his anger—it was that scalawag, Harry Robards. "I–I'm sorry, Margaret. I know I came on pretty strong, but the fact is, Harry Robards has a bit of a reputation in this town, one I don't think you'd want your name linked to."

"Why, Mikal Lee," she said with a coquettish grin, "I do believe you're jealous!"

"Of course I'm not! It's just that. . ."

"And you're the one who told me I should get out and socialize more. Well, I think that was a good piece of advice, and I'm going to try to follow it." Margaret was delighted to watch Mikal's discomfort. Could it possibly be that he really was jealous?

With that delightful possibility in mind, she turned back to her work. "I'm afraid you'll have to excuse me now. I really do have a lot to finish before the shop opens."

❧

Midway through the afternoon, a young boy entered the shop, his arms filled with beautiful, long-stemmed red roses. "For Miss Porter," he said, and handed them to Margaret.

Margaret's heart leaped with joy. She took the roses and went in search of a container for them. She laid aside the card nestled in their leaves; it could wait until she had the flowers in water. She could easily guess who they were from. Mikal had no doubt repented of his ridiculous behavior this morning and chose this lovely way to apologize. He really was sweet, but she was not going to forgive him too quickly. She was having too much fun holding the upper hand for a change.

She emptied a metal container of thread, transferring it to an empty cardboard box. Then she used her water pitcher to fill the container before arranging her flowers in it. The scent of them filled her shop. Their beautiful petals looked like crimson velvet. She had not received flowers from a gentleman since she had left Savannah.

Smiling, she picked up the card and read, "These roses will look like weeds when placed next to your beautiful face. I am counting the hours until seven. Yours, Harry."

Harry? They were not from Mikal at all! Mikal Lee had probably not given her so much as a thought since he left the shop this morning. Well, if he didn't have time to spend with her, then she knew someone who did!

She would wear her prettiest gown tonight. She would coil her hair in one of the latest fashions she had seen in the new magazines, and she would crush some of the rose petals and rub their fragrance behind her ears. She didn't need the attention of Mikal Lee to make her feel wanted. Not when there was a man like Harry Robards to escort her about town!

❧

Sitting next to Harry in the cozy booth of the Silver Saddle's dining room, Margaret took in all of her elegant surroundings. She could hear raucous laughter coming from an adjoining hall and wondered just what kind of establishment Harry had chosen for their evening meal.

He continued to wear that maddening half smile that left her wondering what he had on his mind. "What would you like to drink?" he asked her.

"I'm a tea drinker myself. I know that coffee is more

popular in this area, but old habits are hard to break."

"Tea it is then." He gave the order to the scantily clad wait-ress and ordered something for himself—something that Margaret did not recognize by name.

He leaned very close to her when he spoke, and Margaret felt a bit uneasy in his presence. She had never been out with such a worldly gentleman before, and she had never been in an establishment that was anything like the Silver Saddle.

Harry Robards was a mystery to her, but there was no denying that he did know how to make her feel like a lady. "You said that you had some important business to discuss," she said.

"I do. But I make it a point never to discuss business while I'm eating."

Margaret blushed. She had been raised on strict southern etiquette, and she should not have needed Harry Robards to remind her of it. "Of course. Neither do I." She picked up her oyster fork and began on her appetizer.

Although the food was of gourmet quality, complemented by the elaborate ambience of the dining room, Margaret found it hard to swallow. How could she eat when Harry never took his eyes from her? At last, after she managed to eat enough to satisfy her good manners, she crushed her napkin and laid her utensils in a straight line across her plate.

Harry took much longer to finish his meal, savoring big bites cut from a thick, rare steak. When he, too, had finished, he suggested that they retire to an adjoining room.

He ushered her into a small private room, and Margaret began to be wary of his intentions. "Harry, I really think we should go outside. I enjoy the evening air. . ."

"Margaret!" He spoke her name almost like a caress. "Don't be nervous with me. I have no devious plans to try to seduce a lovely lady such as you. I brought you here so that we could have a private discussion about something that has been on my mind ever since I first set eyes on you."

"A new business venture?"

"Well, I suppose some might consider it that. But before I tell you about it, I want you to promise not to toss my idea aside without giving it some serious thought. I don't want your answer tonight. Will you promise to think about it during the coming week?"

Now Margaret's curiosity hit a new peak. What kind of idea was Harry going to unfold for her? She was perfectly happy in her present millinery business, but of course, she would agree to think about anything he told her. She certainly would not refuse to at least think about his ideas. "Yes, I'll promise. Now, tell me before I die of curiosity."

Harry slipped to the floor on his knees in front of her chair so that their eyes were parallel. "Margaret, I want you to marry me."

Margaret's eyes popped wide, and she gasped, "Harry! You can't be serious! Why, you don't even know me! Is this your idea of a joke?"

"Hardly. I've given the matter a great deal of thought. You see, Margaret, I need a wife."

"In other words, you want me to come keep house for you and cook and bear a bunch of children for you, is that it?" She was furious at his proposal, and she rose to leave.

"Wait, Margaret. It's not like that at all. Remember you promised to think about my idea, and you haven't really heard it all yet."

Margaret slid back into her chair. It was true, she had promised. "Go ahead, but I can already tell you that the answer is no."

"I want an attractive wife to appear by my side in public, to accompany me on my travels, and to share the good life that I lead. As to the cooking and cleaning, I already have people hired to do those things. You would not have to lift one of your pretty fingers. And you would never have to make another bonnet in your entire life, unless you wanted to. You can spend your days shopping in the finest salons in New Orleans or anywhere your heart desires. Money would not be a problem. As for the children, I am not particularly fond of them, but I suppose if you wanted. . ."

"Harry Robards, you don't want a wife; you want a business partner. All this talk about appearing in public and living the good life, you have not said one word about love. Don't you think love is important in a marriage?"

Harry threw back his head and laughed. "Indeed I do! So it's romance you want. Well, I will see that you're not disappointed there, either!"

Margaret understood his implications and felt the blood rush to her face. "Please, Harry. Will you take me home now?"

"Your wish is my command, my dear. Now, and for as long as you like. Just remember your promise, and I'll ask for your answer one week from tonight."

Margaret's head was spinning. Harry held her elbow and led her out the door and into the waiting carriage. He gave an order to the driver and jumped in beside her.

"Margaret, when you've had time to consider the benefits of my proposal, I think you'll realize that you have a rare opportunity for a rich, full life. I'm not an abusive person; I'd do my best to make you happy."

She could not form the words to answer him. This had truly been the most remarkable evening of her entire life, and one she would never forget.

When they drew up to her door, he helped her from the carriage. "Give me your key and I'll unlock for you." He took her key and gave it a turn in the lock, but his hand remained on the knob, barring her entrance. He placed his free arm around her waist and bent to kiss her.

"No, Harry." She twisted out of his grasp and pushed open her door. "Thank you for a–a very interesting evening."

seventeen

Margaret had little difficulty living up to her promise to "think about" Harry's proposal. Not that she wanted to think of it, but how could she not when the idea had been so preposterous? And to make sure that she did not forget, Harry continued to send her roses, fresh ones every day, so that by the middle of the week both upstairs and down reeked of the their odor!

Although Margaret was flattered by all this attention, she considered the flowers a wild extravagance. What would life be like married to a man like Harry? Was there no limit to his wealth? She wondered how he ever came to have so much money. That was just one of the questions she planned to ask him next time they met.

She had not seen Mikal all week. She had sold at least a dozen of his books. Besides bringing in additional income, the books also brought in a whole new line of customers. Now there were almost as many men as women walking through her door.

One day she looked up from her work to see a small, plainly dressed woman standing at the counter. She did not look at all like Margaret's usual stylish clientele, but she wore a pleasant smile on her face.

"How may I help you?" Margaret asked, moving to the counter. "Were you looking for a bonnet or a book?"

"Oh, neither, ma'am. I–I just wanted to stop in to meet you. You see, I'm Alex's mother, and he speaks so highly of you. I wanted to thank you for being so kind to him."

"I'm very glad to meet you, Mrs.—?"

"McCutcheon. America McCutcheon, but my friends just call me Amy."

"Then I shall call you Amy, too, and you must call me Margaret. Alex is such a help to me. I don't know how I could have managed without him."

"He's a good boy," Amy agreed. "I–I don't suppose you'd be needing any more help, would you? I mean, with your bonnets and all. I'm very good with a needle, and you wouldn't have to pay me much." Her eyes took on a pleading look, and Margaret could read unspoken pain in her words.

"Actually, I could use some help, but the truth is, Amy, I really couldn't afford to pay you much of anything. You see, most of the money I make here belongs to the two men who own this building, to pay for the rent, you know, and by the time I pay my own living expenses, there's not a lot left over. Still, I'd like to talk to you. Why don't you take off your coat and we'll have a cup of tea together?"

While Amy removed her coat, Margaret started back to the woodstove in the corner to put on a kettle of water, but before she took two steps, her door opened and in walked two of her best customers. "I'm sorry, Amy. I'm afraid I'll have to take care of business first."

Margaret began to talk to her customers, showing them some new designs from the latest magazines. "These are very popular in New York now, I hear."

The ladies bent their heads over the magazine, and from the corner of her eye, Margaret saw that Amy had gone to the back of the store and put the kettle of water on the stove.

While the ladies were debating about the bonnets, a gentleman came in and was eyeing the books, but Margaret could not ignore her customers to wait on him.

Without so much as a blink of the eye, Amy stepped up to the gentleman and asked, "Could I show you something in books, sir?"

"Well, I do want something for my library. Do you have a recommendation?"

Amy's eyes traveled over the books, and as though she had done so a dozen times before, she pulled a volume from the shelf. "John James Audubon's *Birds of America* is very popular now. We have three volumes here, and I understand he's planning to publish a fourth soon."

Margaret could not hide her surprise. *I hope she knows what she's talking about! If she does, she knows something that I don't!*

The gentleman purchased all three volumes and asked to have the fourth reserved for him if it should come in. Amy found pencil and paper on one of the tables and recorded his name and address. She wrapped his purchases and took his money. "Thank you, sir. Do come back in again."

"I will," he said as he walked to the door. "You can count on it."

Margaret's customers decided to wait to place their orders after picking up some swatches from their dressmaker. "We want to make sure our hats go well with our new gowns," one of them explained. "We'll be back tomorrow."

When they were alone again, Amy gave Margaret the money she had collected for the sale of the books. "Where did you learn so much about books?" Margaret asked her over a cup of freshly brewed tea.

"I've always loved to read. We have that nice new library across town, and I go there whenever I can. I especially like the nature books."

"Amy, I can see that you would be a great help to me. Mind you, I couldn't pay much, but I'll do the best I can, and if we can bring in more money by having two of us here, then in time I could probably do a little better for you."

"Oh, thank you, Margaret. Could I begin right away?"

Margaret laughed. "Amy, I think you already have."

৯৯

John Gorrie folded his plans and put them in his desk drawer. "Mikal, I think with the work we've done these last four days, we have the beginning of a great project. I shall have construction of Trinity Church started in New York at once, and if you think you could bring the whole structure down in four trips on the *Windsong*, then it's my guess that we'll be worshipping in a beautiful new sanctuary by the end of 1838."

Mikal sat across the desk with his head propped on his hand, weary but proud. "This will be the most magnificent piece of architecture in the South when we're done. People will come from all over just to see it. You're to be congratulated, John."

"Don't congratulate me until it's done. By the way, how's that little lady doing with her millinery shop? Last time I looked in, I was amazed at the way her business is building up."

"Yes, Margaret is an amazing woman," Mikal agreed. "I've been wanting to talk to you about her."

"Do I detect a hint of romance in the air?" John said with a smile. He had not failed to notice the way Mikal's eyes glistened every time he spoke her name.

"John, you know I can't even think of romance. I'll admit my feelings for Margaret have grown far stronger than I ever intended, but it wouldn't be fair to encourage her to care for me when I know that I can never marry."

"Never marry? Why, that's preposterous! You're young and healthy, and I can't think of one good reason why you would not consider marriage to the right woman. Of course, who's to say if she's the right one for you? That's something between you and God, and of course, the lady herself."

"I'm afraid it's not that simple. You know what a sailor's life is like, John. What kind of husband and father would I make? No, I wouldn't take on the responsibilities of a family unless I could give them the kind of home they would have a right to expect."

"I agree that you might have to make compromises, but if a man and woman love each other, they will find a way to work things out together. And if Margaret is the woman God has chosen to be your wife, He will show you the way."

Mikal gave his friend a sidelong grin. "For a bachelor, you seem to have a lot of advice on love and marriage."

"Don't laugh; I may have some news to share myself before too much longer. I've been seeing a very charming young widow, and I have some of the same concerns as you about prioritizing my time. But I can tell you right now that I don't plan to live alone for the rest of my life. If Caroline will have me, I plan to propose to her before the year is out."

"I can't wait to meet her. She must be quite a lady to catch the eye of a confirmed old bachelor like you!"

"Indeed she is quite a lady!"

❧

Mikal walked aimlessly through the dark streets toward the docks, his hands in his pockets. He was tired, but he did not feel ready to go back to the boardinghouse where he kept a room. He needed time to think, and he found it easier to think with a clearer head when he could breathe in the fresh, salty air from the bay. He did not know what to do. He had forced himself to stay away from Margaret, although he longed to see her, touch her, breathe the fragrance of her beauty. Knowing that she was less than a mile away only made things more difficult for him.

Margaret deserved a man who could shower her with love and attention, a man who would be there for her when she needed him. He just hoped she was smart enough not to be taken in by the dubious charms of a man like Harry Robards.

The very thought of Harry with his arms around his Margaret made Mikal's blood boil. *Wait a minute! She's not my*

Margaret at all. And she let me know in no uncertain terms that I had no claim on her life. Oh, please, God. Don't let Margaret fall in love with Harry Robards! If I can't have her for my own, then please find her the kind of man who will treat her kindly and make her happy.

Mikal had reached the shoreline, and he reached down to pick up a broken shell. He gave it a mighty fling and watched in the moonlight as it skipped across the water. Tonight he had finally admitted to himself what he had known for a very long time. He was hopelessly in love with Margaret Porter.

eighteen

With Amy helping in the millinery shop, Margaret was able to commit herself to almost twice as many bonnet orders as she could have hoped to finish alone. Although Margaret herself still did the designing and the intricate finishing details, Amy was careful and quick with cutting and basic construction, and her knowledge of books was a real plus.

Amy had even found time to cut out a new calico work dress for Margaret and promised that when it was finished she would try her hand at copying one of the Godey designs from a magazine. Margaret, who had not had a new dress since she arrived in Apalachicola, found this exciting.

Tomorrow night she was dining again with Harry Robards, and she knew that he was expecting to receive her answer to his proposal. Margaret remembered the girl she used to be a year ago, a young and foolish debutante who might have been swayed by Harry's wealth and charm. Even now, she had to admit that the prospect of choosing such a life of luxury presented a temptation. She did not love Harry, and she knew that he did not really love her, but would it be so terribly wrong to marry a man who was willing to take care of her for the rest of her life? Certainly, this was better than being a mail-order bride like Lucy White. At least, she knew what Harry looked like, and he did treat her with respect and dignity. Lucy had told her that if she sincerely put her heart into a marriage, love would grow as time went by. But how could she expect to ever grow to love Harry when deep in her heart she knew that she loved another?

She had not seen Mikal all week. For all she knew, he might

already be on his way back to New York without giving her so much as a wave good-bye! At times she had thought he was the kindest man on earth, but sometimes he seemed totally heartless. *Oh, God, please don't let Mikal leave without seeing me again!*

It occurred to Margaret that the only time she ever prayed was when she wanted something. God had been very good to her, and yet she had never thought to thank Him for anything. Like a spoiled child, she was always asking, and then asking for more.

She looked at her helper, bent over the cutting table. "Amy, do you go to church?"

Amy straightened and rubbed her lower back with her hands. "Yes, I do, and I've been aimin' to ask you if you wanted to come along. Alex and I go to that little church on the corner every Sunday and to prayer meeting on Wednesday nights. Would you like to go with us next Sunday?"

"I might," Margaret said. "I'm afraid I've neglected my spiritual life for a long time. Do you think it's too late for me to change?"

Amy walked over and put an arm across her shoulders. "Margaret, it's never too late for Jesus. Even when we're not looking for Him, He's always standing there knocking, waiting for us to let Him in. You don't even have to wait until Sunday. You could give Him your heart right here and now."

"I—I don't know, Amy. I'm not sure I'm ready to make a full commitment. I need time to think about this. I have so much on my mind right now, but I would like to go to church with you and Alex on Sunday."

"Alex and I will keep you in our prayers." Amy gave her shoulder a little squeeze and returned to her work with a smile on her face.

Margaret picked up her feather duster and began to flick it over the books and shelves. She had so many important decisions to make, and one of them loomed only a day and a half away.

A voice behind her said, "Could I buy a book today, ma'am?"

Margaret felt a rush of blood to her face. Mikal could not fool her; she would recognize his voice even in a crowd. Her knees felt like wet cardboard as she turned to greet him, and a shiver ran through her body.

"Good morning." Her tone was crisp and polite, just as it was for any other customer who entered the shop. She must not let him think that she cared one iota about his absence all week, or that she had even noticed.

"Is that all?" he asked. "Just 'good morning'?"

"What were you expecting me to say?" Margaret could feel the crimson heat in her cheeks, and no amount of effort on her part could prevent it.

"Oh, maybe just something like, 'It's good to see you' or 'How are you today?' "

"It's good to see you. How are you today?" In spite of herself, Margaret had to laugh, especially when she heard Mikal's own infectious laughter.

"Did all these pretty roses come from your garden? I didn't even know that you had a green thumb!"

"Come over here and meet Amy," she said, ignoring his question about the flowers. She grabbed his hand and dragged him across the room. "This is Alex's mother, and she's our newest employee. Amy, this is Mikal, my, uh, business partner."

"How do you do, Amy? Well, this calls for a celebration," Mikal said, "and I know just the place. There's an open-air pavilion down on the waterfront that has a big clambake on the beach every Friday night. They boil shrimp, too, and everybody has a grand time. Why don't I take the two of you and Alex, and we'll all go down there and sample their wares tomorrow night?"

Amy looked to Margaret for her cue, and Margaret felt her

face grow hot again. "It sounds very nice, Mikal, but I—I have already made plans for tomorrow night."

"I see," Mikal said with a clipped tone. His smile dropped, and he turned his attention back to the bookshelf to avoid meeting her eyes. "It looks as though I need to bring more books next time I come. I'll just take an inventory of what's left, so I'll know what to buy."

He busied himself with the books while Margaret continued with her dusting. Amy returned to the cutting table, and an awkward silence enveloped the room. After several minutes, Mikal turned back to Margaret and said, "Now that you have Amy here to wait on the customers, could you manage to slip away for a few minutes? We could go down to the café and have a cup of coffee or tea, if you prefer——or have you already made plans for the morning as well?"

Margaret ignored his biting sarcasm. "I do not have plans for this morning, Mikal. I will get my wrap."

ða

Sitting across from him at the same table where they had eaten oysters on one of their happier days, Margaret tried to keep her teacup from shaking in her hands. She was determined to keep their conversation pleasant and impersonal. "Have you and John been successful with your planning this week?"

"Yes, I think so. Look, Margaret, I—"

"And what do you think of Amy? She's such a big help to me. I think her help will more than compensate for the small salary she earns."

"That's good. Now, Margaret—"

"Her real name is America. America McCutcheon. I suppose she's of Scottish ancestry. So many of the ladies around here are, you know."

"Stop it, Margaret. You know as well as I do that we did not come here to talk about Amy's ancestry. I want to talk about our relationship."

"Our relationship? Do we have one, Mikal?"

"Well, of course we do. We have a–a *business* relationship, and it is very important to me that we establish a good reputation in this town." Mikal's words were not coming out the way he intended, because the truth was that he had no idea just what message he intended to convey. He only knew that he must find some way to keep Margaret out of the arms of Harry Robards.

"Just what are you implying, Mikal? Do you feel that I am threatening the reputation of our *business* relationship?" Her green eyes flashed fire. When she saw him spluttering for a reply, she saved him the effort. "I know exactly where this conversation is going, Mikal. You are upset about my friendship with Harry Robards, and I have already told you that I will choose my own social life. Could we talk about something else?"

"I'm only trying to help you, Margaret. Harry Robards is known around here as a ladies' man. I hope that you are too intelligent to fall for his fancy clothes and his smooth talk. He's not a man you can trust."

Margaret was furious! Even though she had her own doubts about Harry's integrity, Mikal had no right to interfere in her life. He wanted to stand on the sidelines and call all the shots without getting into the game himself! In a voice as calm as she could muster, she said, "It might interest you to know that Mr. Robards has asked me to be his wife."

"His what?" Mikal jumped up so fast that his coffee cup went flying into the air and landed on the floor in a hundred pieces. In the ensuing confusion, Margaret turned and slipped quietly out the door.

ঌ

Margaret dressed carefully for her dinner with Harry Robards. Her hands shook as she pinned up her hair and fastened her cameo brooch at her neckline. She was wearing her only other fancy gown tonight, not wanting to wear the same thing she had worn the week before. If she did marry Harry, she would soon have a closet full of gowns, new ones every week, and a maid to dress her hair.

She still had a few questions to ask Harry before she gave him her final answer. She was not sure how long his patience would hold out, but she couldn't be rushed into a decision that would affect the rest of her life.

When she finished dressing, she went downstairs to wait for his carriage.

❧

Mikal and John walked along the waterfront, listening to the music and sampling the hot, steamed delicacies from the gulf. "Apalachicola is truly the oyster capital of the world, my friend," John proclaimed, letting one of the delicious creatures slide down his throat. "I've sampled them up and down both coasts, and in Europe as well, but no place has a match for ours."

"Yes," Mikal said, his eyes cast over the white-capped blue waves. He had contributed little to the conversation tonight. He just could not erase the picture from his mind of Margaret and Harry sealing their promise with a kiss.

"What's the matter, Mikal?" John finally asked. "You're not enjoying yourself tonight. Why didn't you bring your lady friend along if you're going to moon over her all evening long?" He smiled and gave Mikal a playful jab in the ribs.

"As a matter of fact, I asked her, but she had already made plans."

"Oh."

"With Harry Robards."

John drew in his breath. "Uh-oh. Now I see what's spoiled your mood. Well, perhaps you misjudged her after all. If she's Harry's type, then she surely isn't yours. You'd be well to be done with her."

Mikal sprang to her defense. "She's not his type at all, John. That's the trouble. She's just so sweet and naïve. I just don't want her to be hurt or taken advantage of."

John looked at Mikal for several minutes. The two men had known each other for a long time, and they were almost as close as brothers. "Mikal, you're in love with that woman. It's written all over your face." When Mikal made no move to deny it, John continued, "Well, you have to do something about it. Have you told her yet? Does she know that you love her?"

"No, of course not. I've already explained to you how I feel about that. I won't ask her to live the lonely life of a sailor's wife. It wouldn't be fair; I love her too much for that."

"So instead, you'd leave her to someone like Harry Robards? Do you think that's where she'll find happiness? Why don't you tell her how you feel and let her make up her own mind about the kind of life she wants to lead? If you really want to be fair to the lady, Mikal, you owe her your total honesty."

"I'd never thought of it in just that way, John, although she has reminded me on several recent occasions that she's capable of making her own decisions. Perhaps you're right, but that still doesn't settle the other issue."

"What issue is that?"

"Margaret has still not committed her life to Christ. You know what the Scriptures say about being unequally yoked. She is reading the Bible now. I've tried to lead her in the right direction, but unless she makes her own decision, it means nothing."

John walked along in silence for several minutes, contemplating his answer. Finally he spoke. "My friend, I do not know if Margaret Porter is the woman God has intended for you or not. You are riding through a turbulent sea right now, but if you put your faith in Christ and trust Him, He will steer you on the right course."

nineteen

The horses' hooves clip-clopped down the wide brick avenue.
Margaret sat next to Harry in the velvet-lined carriage, allow-
ing him to hold her hand.

"You've had all week to think about this, Margaret. I've tried
to be patient, but I can't be dangled like a fish on a hook. I
know many women who would not need even an hour to make
the kind of decision you've been invited to make. What is it
you're trying to resolve? Is there someone else?"

"I'm not 'many women,' Harry. I'm me, Margaret Porter,
and things just seem to be moving too fast for me lately. I feel
as though I'm being whirled around in a cyclone. I guess I just
need more time."

"How much time does it take to say yes?" He squeezed her
hand in the darkness.

"Harry, I still feel that we hardly know each other. Why, do
you realize that I don't even know what line of work you're in?
You've never told me what you do."

"Women should not have to worry about unromantic things
like a man's work. I promise that you'll be well provided for.
You will be a real-life Cinderella, my dear.

"I've built a beautiful new home on the bluff overlooking the
river, fully staffed with competent servants, and I want someone to share it with me. I need a sophisticated wife who can
sit at the end of my table making intelligent conversation
when I entertain, and I'm willing to share my name and my
wealth with her. You, my dear, are the first woman I have ever
asked to do me that honor."

"That's all very flattering, Harry, but I'd still like to know how do you make your living? Will you be away from home, traveling a lot?"

"I'll be away a bit. And you'll be free to travel, too. New England, Europe, the *world* will be at your doorstep. But this is the last time I am going to ask you, Margaret. Harry Robards is not a beggar. I will wait until tomorrow for your answer, but no longer. You've had ample time to reach a decision, and I must get on with my life."

"You're right, Harry. You've been very tolerant of my indecisiveness. Just let me sleep on it one more night. Come by my shop in the morning and I will give you my answer."

The carriage slowed and then stopped in front of Margaret's Millinery Shoppe, and this time when Harry drew her into his arms, she let him kiss her. His lips touched hers lightly at first, and she waited for the tingling sensation she had experienced when Mikal kissed her beneath the oaks in Tampa. But this time there was no sensation at all, and when his kisses grew more passionate and demanding, it set off an alarm in her head so that she placed her hands on his chest and pushed him away. "Stop, Harry. I–I have to go in now."

Harry groaned. "You certainly know how to tease a man, Margaret. But we will soon have things settled between us. You won't get to tease me anymore." He winked and gave her a salacious grin. She slipped her key into the lock and pushed open her door. "Good night, Harry."

⋙

Margaret snuggled beneath her blanket and let the events of the night play back through her mind. She was aware that Harry had never answered her questions about his occupation. What could he possibly be involved in that he would not want her to know about? Did he really only want to shield her from the everyday concerns of his work as he said, or did he have something to hide?

And there was another matter. If she was seriously thinking

of spending the rest of her life with this man, then why did his kisses have so little effect on her? Could she learn to love Harry Robards the way Lucy White had learned to love her mail-order husband?

She tossed and turned for hours, and sleep eluded her until just before dawn. When she finally did drift off, her sleep was invaded by puzzling dreams. She sat in a strange dining room at the end of a very long table. A staff of uniformed servants circled the table, serving her guests exotic dishes. But the puzzling part was that the man who sat at the head of the table had neither sleek, black hair nor a mustache. He was clean shaven, and his hair was as blond as fine corn silk, curling softly where it met the edge of his collar.

&

Who could ever have predicted the bedlam that was to take place in Margaret's Millinery Shoppe the next morning? Amy arrived early and went right to work at the cutting table. She explained to Margaret that Alex would be in a little late this morning. Since it was Saturday, she decided to let him sleep in for a change, but he would be along soon to do his chores.

Next Mikal arrived, looking at once pleased and agitated. Margaret noticed dark circles beneath his eyes and wondered if he noticed the ones that must be under hers.

Pulling Margaret aside, he said, "I must speak to you in private."

"Can it wait? I have to help Amy finish some work and get ready to open the shop at eight. We'll have customers coming in here in less than an hour, and there is so much yet to be done."

"All right. I'll look through the books again, but as soon as you get a minute, I'd like to take you outside where we can talk."

Margaret and Amy worked fast and furiously. Amy finished her cutting and swept up the scraps from beneath the cutting table, salvaging any pieces big enough for later use as trimming. Margaret used her needle and thread to add a bunch of yellow flowers to a green bonnet she had promised to have ready for Mrs. Raney this morning.

"We'd better unlock the door," Amy said. "There are already two ladies standing outside waiting to get in."

Amy opened the door and welcomed them into the shop. "Come in, ladies." And then she looked up to see the big carriage that had stopped just in front of her shop. "Oh, no!"

Harry Robards stepped down from the carriage, carrying his gold-tipped cane. He sprinted up to her door.

Just as Harry opened the door and started to walk through, Alex came running in at top speed, bumping against Harry's leg in his hurry to attend to his chores. "Sorry I'm—"

"Just where do you think you're going, young man?" Harry jerked the boy up by his shirt collar, and Alex dangled like an ornament on a Christmas tree, his brown eyes bulging with fright.

Before the child could answer, Harry headed him toward the door. "You little street urchins have no business coming into a shop like this. Be gone with you!" He shoved him roughly toward the door.

Alex, his eyes brimming with tears, turned back to protest. "But sir, I *work* here! I'm the boy that delivered your—"

"Work? I know your kind. The only work you ever do is steal from respectable people. Get out of here, I said." With that, he used his boot to send the boy sprawling outside onto the sidewalk.

By now, the two lady customers had crowded toward the back of the store, blocking Margaret and Amy's view so that at first they did not understand what had happened. But when realization set in, everything broke loose at once.

Amy screamed, *"Alex! My baby!"*

Margaret, with fire in her eyes, started toward Harry. "Don't you dare lay a hand on that child!" But before she could make her way across the room to where he stood, Mikal whipped around and grabbed Harry by the lapels of his brass-buttoned waistcoat. "You big bully!" He balled his right hand into a fist and swung, catching Harry just below the chin. Harry reeled and fell. Mikal stood back and waited for him to stand up again, but when he did, Margaret jumped right in the middle between the two angry men. "Stop it! Both of you! What is the meaning of this?"

Amy had retrieved her son from the street and was washing the tear-streaked dirt from his face.

Harry used his handkerchief to wipe blood from his chin. "Margaret, I was trying to eject that thieving little urchin from your store when this—" he glared at Mikal, "this ruffian from the waterfront—"

Mikal drew back to swing again, but Margaret stood her ground to prevent it. "Harry, that little boy you referred to as a thieving urchin is the son of a very dear friend of mine. He does odd jobs for me, and I think you owe him an apology."

"Now, look here, Margaret. If I made a mistake, I'm sorry. I was only trying to help you."

"She doesn't need the help of a riverboat gambler, Robards, so why don't you just take your fancy cane and get out of here."

"We'll let my fiancée decide about that," Harry said. "Go ahead and tell them, my dear."

Mikal looked as though someone had just punched him in the stomach. His face paled as his shoulders slumped, and he looked to Margaret for an explanation. "Yes," he said. "By all means. Tell me."

Margaret looked at Amy and Alex and at the two women customers cowering in the back corner of her shop. Then she looked from Mikal to Harry, letting her eyes linger on Harry for a long time. At last she spoke. "There is nothing to tell.

Nothing at all. I am no one's fiancée, and I want both of you men out of my store at once, do you hear? You are frightening my customers and my help, and I will not stand for it. If you want to fight like gutter trash, then go outside and do it in the streets, but not in my shop."

She used all of the strength her one hundred ten pounds could muster and gave the two big men a hearty shove toward the door.

"I'm so sorry, ladies," she apologized to her customers. "What can I show you today?"

"I–I'm afraid we'll have to come back another day," one of the ladies said, fluttering her hands nervously. "We–we really must be going." The two women hurried toward the door, furtively looking in each direction as though they expected a momentary attack. "Well, I never!" Margaret heard one of them say as they pushed through the doorway to the sidewalk. She wondered if they would ever return.

"Amy," Margaret said, trying to still the quaver in her voice, "why don't you take the rest of the day off. Take Alex home and get him cleaned up. We aren't likely to be so busy that I can't handle things here for the rest of the day."

"I hate to leave you alone," Amy protested, but she began to gather up her things as she spoke. "Are you sure you don't want me to come back in after dinner?"

"No, Amy, you deserve a day off after all you've been through this morning. I used to handle this shop alone every day until you came along, and I'm sure I can manage for one afternoon."

As Alex and his mother moved toward the door, Margaret laid a hand on Amy's arm. "Do you remember that you invited me to come to Sunday service at your church?"

"Of course I remember. So will you come, Margaret? Oh, please say you will."

"I think I'd like that, Amy. I've been wrestling with some

important decisions about my life, and I think it's high time I put them into action."

Amy gave her friend a quick hug. She turned to leave, but not before Margaret saw the glistening of a tear in her eye.

twenty

Late in the afternoon, Margaret was bent over her worktable cutting a bonnet from a piece of emerald moiré taffeta that Mikal had brought from New York. The shop seemed lonely without Amy, and Margaret hummed to break the silence.

She stood to stretch, placing her palms on her lower back. Perhaps she would close early this evening. This had been such a trying day!

Looking toward the street, she was surprised to see the now familiar carriage of Harry Robards pulling to a stop outside her door for the second time that day. She turned and busied herself arranging the hats and bonnets on her shelf so that she would not have to face him until he spoke. She heard the bell on the door jingle, but still she did not look up.

"Good afternoon, Margaret." Harry waited for her reply, and when none was forthcoming, he continued. "I stopped for two reasons. First, I wanted to say again how sorry I was that our . . .um. . .conversation this morning was so rudely interrupted by that unfortunate. . .um. . .experience. I'm sure that by now you've had time to think the matter through and realize that I was only trying to act in your best interest."

She whipped around and glared at him in astonishment, her eyes blazing sparks of fire. "My best interest? By abusing an innocent child?"

"My dear, you are so young and naïve, which just proves my point that you need someone who can take care of you. In time you will learn not to underestimate these children of the streets. They know how to use their juvenile charm as a cover-up for their mischief." He held up both palms to stifle her protest. "Oh, I know they can be quite winsome and cunning, but—"

She cut him off before he could continue. "What was the second thing you came to say, Harry?"

"I want to tell you that I am leaving tomorrow on an extended business trip."

"To pursue your gambling career?" Her words dripped icicles.

He was momentarily astonished, but he quickly regained his composure. "Yes, Margaret, I'm a gambler; a very successful one, I might add. I've never denied that. Do you find that idea so distasteful?"

"*Distasteful*? I find it *reprehensible* that you prey on those less fortunate to support your flamboyant lifestyle." She thought of her own father and the downfall gambling had brought him to.

"That is a very narrow viewpoint, my dear. I do not force others into the games of chance, and if I am rewarded for my skill and knowledge, then that is my good fortune."

"I won't argue the point, Harry. Is that the last thing you came to tell me?"

"As I started to tell you before we got sidetracked, I am leaving Apalachicola on Monday morning. I am taking a steamboat to the beautiful city of New Orleans. I had hoped that you would go with me and that this might be our wedding trip. But I told you once before that Harry Robards does not beg. This is either to be our wedding trip or this is good-bye, Margaret."

He hooked his thumbs into the pockets of his waistcoat and waited for her answer. The confident expression on his face told Margaret that he had little doubt as to what her decision would be.

Margaret looked beyond the shop window and saw the elegant carriage waiting outside. She shifted her gaze to Harry, tall and debonair in his fancy clothes. She closed her eyes and saw her life as it could be—filled with dazzling parties and stylish clothes, servants, trips, and all the extravagances that money could buy.

The silence in the room was as thick as a winter fog, so that Margaret could hear the beats of her own racing heart.

She opened her eyes and looked squarely into Harry's confident face. She drew a deep breath before she whispered, "Good-bye, Harry."

His jaw dropped in disbelief before his dark eyes pierced hers with a menacing glare. "You," he said, pointing his finger in her face, "are making a grave mistake." His sinister tone made Margaret's flesh crawl as she watched him turn and stalk out of her shop.

☙

Margaret sat beside Amy and Alex near the front of the small church, barely able to contain her excitement. This was the day she was going to make a public declaration of her faith and give her heart to the Lord. She had thought and prayed long and hard about her decision.

When the congregation stood to sing the hymn "Amazing Grace," Amy grasped Margaret's hand and gave it a gentle squeeze. "I once was lost but now am found, was blind but now I see."

The minister read from his big pulpit Bible, from the thirteenth chapter of Acts. "Be it known unto you therefore, men and brethren, that through this man is preached unto you the forgiveness of sins: And by him all that believe are justified from all things."

The words were familiar to Margaret because she had read them over and over again from the black leather Testament Mikal had given to her. She understood at last what Mikal had wanted her to know all along, that Jesus had already paid the price for her sins and that He loved her just as she was and had a place prepared for her in God's kingdom.

She listened as the minister's words washed over her like a warm summer shower, healing, comforting, refreshing. And when at last he issued an invitation from the pulpit, Margaret made her way down the aisle as tears washed her cheeks.

Amy and Alex stood beside her as she made her profession of faith before the congregation. Margaret thought her heart would burst with happiness. Her only regret was that Mikal was not here to share in the wonder and greatness of this moment.

⁂

Much later, snuggled beneath her patchwork quilt, Margaret reread the passage from Acts by the dim light of her candle. Wonder of wonders, she was now a true child of God, and nothing in this world could ever separate her from His love.

twenty-one

Margaret awoke at first light with a song in her heart. "Amazing grace, how sweet the sound that saved a wretch like me!" The very air she breathed seemed somehow different, cleaner, fresher! She was a new creation! She could hardly wait to see Mikal and share her joy.

Mikal! Saturday she had tossed him out like a bad apple, and tomorrow was the day he was due to set sail for New York. Surely he would come by to see her before he left town. Or maybe he wouldn't, after the harsh words she had flung at him. She couldn't bear the thought of his leaving without resolving their disagreement of the day before.

Of course, Mikal had been wrong to resort to violence to settle the dispute with Harry Robards, but his motives were so valorous that she could hardly point a finger of blame.

Poor little Alex! He must have been terrified when Harry grabbed him like that without any warning. She would give him a small little treat when he came to do his chores this morning.

She stirred a pan of oatmeal over the one burner of her iron stove and tossed in a handful of raisins to make it special. Knowing this to be one of Alex's favorite foods, she planned to pour a generous scoop of molasses over the top and insist that he eat a nice, warm bowl of it before he went to school.

Margaret slipped into the new calico dress that Amy had made for her and ran a brush over her hair. Oh, she did so hope that Mikal would come into the shop this morning!

She could hear Alex banging on the front door and hurried down the stairs to let him in. "My, but you're early today!"

"Yes'm. I didn't get everything done," he explained, lowering his eyes sheepishly, "so I thought I'd come early and do some extra today."

Margaret wanted to hug him, but she knew that to do so would only embarrass him all the more. "I'm so fortunate to have such a dependable worker," she said. "By the way, Alex, when you go upstairs, there's a pan of oatmeal on the stove for you. I put lots of raisins in it, and I poured molasses over the top. Stop and have a bowl of it before you begin your chores."

His face brightened with a wide smile. "Yes'm, I'd like that. Thank you, Miss Margaret."

She watched him scamper up the staircase before she turned to her worktable. Mrs. Raney hadn't come in on Saturday, but she would be coming in this morning for her new bonnet, and Margaret still needed to sew the ties on it. In the chaos, she'd forgotten about it. Then she'd become so busy she hadn't had time to do it. Margaret pushed a silver thimble onto the middle finger of her right hand and chose a needle from her pin cushion.

When she heard the front door open, she called without looking up, "Come in, Amy. You're early this morning, too."

But the footsteps were too heavy for those of her assistant. Her first thought was that it might be Mikal Lee, and she jumped up with a smile on her face. But when she saw the tall, dark Harry Robards towering over her, her breath caught in her throat. "Harry! What are you doing here this morning? I thought you were leaving town today."

"I am." He leered at her. "And you, my dear, are going to New Orleans with me." He reached down and grasped her arm. "Come along, now. Our carriage is waiting."

"I'm not going anywhere with you!" She tried to jerk away from his grip, but he twisted her arm behind her and pulled up on it until she cried out in pain. "Stop, Harry! You're hurting me!"

Harry gave a low, guttural chuckle and pushed her toward the door ahead of him. "I'm not hurting you; you're hurting yourself by your foolish resistance. Come along now like a good girl, and everything will be just fine."

Outside, he lifted her up and fairly threw her into his carriage. "Please," she called, trying to attract the attention of the driver, but he turned a deaf ear to his passengers and began to move through the streets of Apalachicola toward the waterfront.

"Are you out of your mind, Harry Robards? You may be strong enough to overpower me, but you cannot force me to marry you."

Harry guffawed. "Marriage, my dear, is no longer one of your options."

"Then what. . . ?"

"You had your chance for marriage with all the trimmings that would have turned you into a fine lady, but you chose to decline my offer. I did not look kindly on your rejection, so from here on out, the choices are all mine."

Margaret's stomach tied itself in knots. If only there had been someone in the shop to witness her abduction and send for help, but now she had no one to call on. Or did she?

Dear Lord, she prayed silently, *I don't know what to do! I don't see any way out of this trouble, so I'm turning the whole thing over to You. Please help me!* She was not alone; Jesus had promised to be with her to the end. A gentle warmth spread through her being as she sensed her Savior's presence. She did not know what was in store for her in the hours and days ahead, but whatever happened, she knew that she would never be alone again.

Feeling her muscles relax within his grip, Harry eyed her suspiciously.

"Harry, where are you taking me?" The hysteria was gone from her voice now, and she spoke to him calmly. "Can't you see that what you're doing is wrong?"

The sinister smirk never left his face. "I've already told you where we're going. Have you forgotten already? New Orleans is a wonderful city, filled with gaiety and excitement. It's a pity you declined to go there as my wife. The alternative will not be nearly so pretty."

Margaret understood his implications, and the horror of them threatened to relieve her stomach of the breakfast she had enjoyed earlier. She considered her options. The carriage was moving so swiftly that there was no chance that she could jump out, even if Harry loosened his grip. If she screamed, who would hear her? And even if someone did, the chances were strong that she and Harry would appear to be only having a lovers' quarrel.

They were approaching the waterfront now, and Margaret could see the big paddle wheeler waiting at the dock. Perhaps if she appeared to be cooperating with Harry, he would let down his guard and a chance for escape would present itself as they boarded the steamer.

"Oh, my!" she exclaimed, struggling to keep her words at an even pitch. "Just look at that! I've never been on a paddle wheeler before."

Harry eyed her curiously, but he said nothing. When they drew up to the dock, he jumped to the ground and lifted Margaret out to stand beside him, keeping a firm grasp on her arm.

Margaret looked from right to left, searching for a familiar face or even a kind and sympathetic one, but everyone she saw seemed to be rushing about, preoccupied with the eminent departure of the *River Queen*.

She forced herself to smile up at Harry, but all her coquettish charms failed to loosen his grip on her arm. Twisting her arm behind her back, he shoved her ahead of him toward the loading ramp.

Soon she would be on board the ship, churning out into the Gulf of Mexico, and her chance for escape would be gone. *It's now or never,* she thought.

As Harry presented two tickets to the steward and pushed her forward, she screamed, "Help me! Someone please help me! This man is taking me against my. . ."

"Now, darling," Harry said, smiling at her as he gave her arm another painful thrust, "you mustn't be afraid." Turning to the astonished steward, he explained, "My little bride has a sudden case of wedding-day nerves, but I suppose you're used to that with honeymooners."

The steward chuckled and gave Harry a conspiratorial wink. "Congratulations, sir. Enjoy your trip."

Margaret stumbled aboard the deck and looked back to see if someone—anyone—had heard her plea and might be coming to help her, but the laughs and whispers proved that Harry had turned the whole dreadful scenario into a cruel and sadistic joke.

He pushed her ahead of him into an outside stateroom and closed the door behind them. "I trust you will be comfortable, my dear."

Margaret was too frightened to appreciate the ornate furnishings of the cabin or the huge bowl of fresh fruit on the table. "What you are doing is criminal, Harry. What do you want of me?"

"Don't look so upset, my dear. I am not such a bad fellow after you get to know me, and you *will* get to know me, Margaret. That was quite a little show you put on outside. Just to make certain you don't try anything like that again, I'll be bringing all your meals into our cabin, and you won't have such an opportunity again."

"*Our* cabin?"

Harry laughed. He was obviously enjoying himself. "Of course. What sort of arrangement were you expecting?" When she did not answer, he continued, "I'm going outside to have a smoke on the deck, but I shall return. Don't try any of your tricks again, Margaret, or I assure you that you'll regret it."

She heard the key turn in the lock when he closed the door. If only there were some way for her to get out before the boat left the shore! She waited for a few moments and then tried the door. Just as she had suspected, it was locked.

Oh, what was she to do? She looked around the cabin for something to work into the keyhole.

Next to the fruit bowl was a plate of cheese and crackers, with a small knife beside it. She had not noticed it before because she had been so repelled by the sight of food. Now she picked up the knife and inserted it into the keyhole. She twisted it first one way and then the other, but the stubborn knob refused to turn in her hand. In frustration, she kicked the door.

She put the knife back on the table in exactly the same spot where she had found it. It would not do for Harry to suspect what she had been trying to do!

How long did it take for a smoke on the deck? He would likely be returning at any minute, unless he found someone to engage in a card game.

Margaret fell to her knees beside the satin-covered bed and prayed from the depths of her heart. When she heard the key in the lock, she did not raise her head. She was sure that Harry would ridicule her pleas to the Almighty, but that did not matter to her one whit. What mattered to her now was that her Lord was with her, and nothing on earth could ever separate her from His love.

Margaret realized now that her whole life had been a quest, but only recently had she come to realize just what she had been searching for. Superficial romance, money, and material possessions had left her feeling incomplete and unsatisfied. Now that she had turned her life over to God, peace and happiness filled her heart. Facing unknown horrors, she placed herself in His hands.

She held her breath as the footsteps moved closer to her side. "The Lord is my shepherd. . ."

"Margaret?"

"Mikal!"

"Shh! We have to get out of here."

"Oh, Mikal, how did you know where. . . ?"

He pulled her to her feet and led her toward the door. "No time for questions now. Just be quiet and follow me." He eased the door open and looked outside in both directions before he pulled her onto the deck beside him. With his arm around her waist, he led her toward the loading ramp.

Margaret's heart pounded as the two of them moved with the stealth of a cat stalking a mouse. They'd almost made it to the ramp when Harry Robards stepped out in front of them.

"You again," Harry snarled. "I'll have you arrested for breaking into my cabin!"

"Yes, do that, Harry. Call the captain. I know him well, and I have a few things I'd like to tell him myself."

Harry's face turned the color of a ripe plum. He looked from Mikal to Margaret and back to Mikal again. He seemed to realize the futility of further protest. "Take her, then. She's not worth the trouble. You two 'holier-than-thou' idiots deserve each other."

Just as Mikal's arm propelled Margaret toward the ramp, a woman's piercing scream split the air. "He's got a gun!"

Mikal pushed Margaret to the floor and fell beside her in one quick motion, just as the shot was fired. Because of his instant reaction, the bullet that was aimed at Mikal's heart barely grazed his left shoulder.

Harry was immediately overpowered by members of the ship's crew and hauled away, his profanities ringing through the air.

Margaret pushed herself to a sitting position and looked at

Mikal's blood-stained shirt. "Oh, Mikal! You're hurt!"

The steward crouched beside them, barking orders to his crew. "Someone call the doctor. Get a stretcher over here!" And to Mikal, he said, "Don't try to move. We'll have you lifted out of here in a moment, and we'll have our ship's doctor take a look at your shoulder. Are you all right, miss?"

"Yes, I'm fine, but. . ."

"I'm fine, too," Mikal said, staggering to his feet. "Just help us get out of here and I'll have my own doctor look at this shoulder. It's only a flesh wound." He balled up his handkerchief and pressed it hard against his shoulder to stem the flow of blood. "Margaret, are you sure you're all right?"

"Oh, Mikal, I've caused you so much trouble. Let the ship's doctor look at you now before you lose any more blood. As soon as he says it's safe, we'll go to find John."

twenty-two

Three people sat in John Gorrie's waiting room, but when the doctor stuck his head through the doorway and saw Mikal and Margaret, he ushered them into his office at once. "What in the world have you been up to now?" he asked, eyeing Mikal's arm in a sling. "I say, for a passive man, you're managing to get yourself into more scrapes lately than the town's worst ruffians! What happened here?"

While John removed the bandages applied by the ship's doctor, Mikal gave a brief explanation. "Fortunately, young Alex was just coming down Margaret's staircase when Harry Robards entered her shop. Not wanting another encounter with the man, the boy crouched on the stairs and saw everything. I was down at the wharf supervising the loading of my cargo when I saw him flying down the road toward me. I knew at once that there must be a real emergency, so I dropped everything and ran to meet him in the street. He told me everything that had happened. Luckily, he heard Harry say something about New Orleans, so I took off for the pier where the *River Queen* was docked."

"But how did you know which cabin I was in?" Margaret asked.

"That part was easy. I know a lot of the crewmen who work on the *River Queen*. I just asked one of them where I might find Mr. Robards, and he directed me to your door. Picking the lock was the tricky part." Mikal chuckled and then grimaced when the movement hurt his shoulder. "I've never been called on to do anything like that before."

The grin that spread across his face melted Margaret's

heart, and she found one more reason to love this wonderful man. He was the one who had directed her to a new life in Christ, and now he had saved her from life-destroying harm at the hands of the evil Harry Robards.

"Looks like the ship's doctor did a good job here, Mikal," John said. "I'll just pour on some of this antiseptic to ward against infection and rewrap it. It's a nasty wound, and it's going to hurt pretty badly for a few days, but your muscles are all intact, and when it heals, you'll be as good as new."

"I'm supposed to sail out of here tomorrow, John."

"Sorry, friend. You're not going anywhere tomorrow. In fact, I'm ordering limited activity for a week. I'll have a room fixed up for you here at my house where I can keep an eye on you for the next few days. We don't want to risk an infection."

Margaret smiled inwardly. Mikal would be in town for at least another week. She had so many things she wanted to tell him before he left again.

"He's going to need a nurse, Margaret," John said with a twinkle in his eye. "Do you suppose you could hang around here during the day and help me take care of him?"

"Now, look here. . ."

"I'm sure I can get Amy to run the shop for a few days," Margaret said before Mikal could finish his protest. "I'll talk to her about it at once."

Mikal uttered a mock groan, and John turned his back to conceal his grin.

☙

Margaret sat on the sofa in John Gorrie's living room and spread her wide calico skirts around her. She let her eyes rest on Mikal, sitting in the chair across from her, and smiled. "John is spoiling us both," she said. "That was a delicious supper."

"Yes, and as soon as he gets back from his round of evening house calls, I'm going to thank him."

"Well, we both thanked him already, but I suppose it wouldn't hurt to thank him again."

"No, that's not what I mean," Mikal said with a wry smile on his lips. "I mean I want to thank him for something else."

When Margaret lifted quizzical brows, he continued. "I want to thank him for keeping you here with me and for giving us this time alone together. There is so much that I want to say to you, Margaret."

He crossed to sit beside her and put his one good arm around her shoulders. "I guess I'm not a very smart man. I had to almost lose you before I realized that I can't live my life without you. I love you, Margaret. I think I've loved you from the moment I first saw you standing on the deck of the *Windsong* with your hair blowing in the wind. I couldn't admit it then, even to myself, because you were pledged to another man. But this afternoon, when you told me the story of your conversion, I knew that you were a part of God's plan for my life, and although I'm going to have to make some adjustments to my lifestyle, I want to marry you and spend the rest of my life trying to make you happy."

"Oh, Mikal! How I've dreamed of hearing you say those words. I think I fell in love with you that same day when we met on the deck of the schooner, but my values were so warped that I wasn't able to see it clearly until much later."

He drew her close to him and kissed her on the forehead, but when she tilted her chin, their lips met in a kiss that was at once both fierce and sweet.

"Does that mean your answer is yes?" he asked her, pulling back to catch his breath.

Her shining eyes met his and a wellspring of joy burst from somewhere deep inside her as she whispered her answer. "Yes! Oh, yes, Mikal Lee. I do love you, and I want us to share the rest of our lives together."

epilogue

On May 22, 1838, Margaret Abigail Porter and Mikal Austin Lee spoke their sacred wedding vows in the recently completed Trinity Church, which was built in New York and brought to Apalachicola in four sections.

The bride was radiant in a gown of white satin. Her attendants were Caroline Gorrie, recent bride of Dr. John Gorrie, and America McCutcheon.

Mr. Lee was attended by Dr. John Gorrie and Master Alex McCutcheon.

After the ceremony, all guests were invited to attend a reception honoring the bride and groom, held at the home of Dr. and Mrs. Gorrie.

Following their wedding trip to New York, Mr. and Mrs. Lee will be at home in their new residence on Concord Street.

※

With their arms wrapped around each other, Margaret and Mikal Lee stood on the swaying deck of the *Windsong,* where they had met just two years before. Today the wind was calm, and the waters of the Atlantic were almost smooth.

"Did you ever imagine on the day we left Savannah together that we would one day be standing here together as man and wife?" Mikal asked her.

Margaret's musical laughter floated on the ocean breeze. "Not in my wildest dreams," she admitted. "And I still can't believe that I am really going to New York with you."

"If my guess is right, this is only the first of many trips we'll be making to New York together while I'm training my new assistant to take over my duties on the *Windsong.* Did you get a list from Amy of all the things she wants us to bring back for the shop?"

"Yes, and our bookshelves, too, are almost empty. We'll have a lot of shopping to do."

"John tells me that the store next to your millinery shop will be vacated in about a month. I've been thinking of remodeling it to connect the two and moving all of our books in there. That would give you more room for your hats and bonnets, and I'd have a whole store just for books. What do you think of that?"

Margaret laid her head on his chest. "I think I have a very smart husband," she said.

Mikal pulled her close and whispered into her hair, "At least I know one thing I've done that was smart, very, very smart!" He used his right forefinger to tilt her chin upward and looked deep into her sparkling green eyes before he bent to place a kiss on the lips of his beautiful bride.

ॐ

APALACHICOLA TODAY

Although the Constitution Convention was held in 1838, Florida did not actually become a state until 1845.

Apalachicola, once the third largest port in the Florida Territory, is now a sleepy little town in Florida's panhandle, where visitors can still take a walk down Market Street, savor the world's most succulent oysters, and watch spectacular sunsets over the Gulf of Mexico. Maps are free at the Chamber of Commerce for a walking tour of the historic district, which is less than two miles square.

Dr. John Gorrie died in 1855 at the age of fifty-two, but not before receiving a patent for mechanical refrigeration. Initially designed to cool his fevered patients, his invention spawned our modern air-conditioning and commercial refrigeration systems. Today his statue stands as the focal point of Apalachicola's Gorrie Square.

Your tour will take you by the home of world-famous botanist Dr. Alvin Chapman and the two-story home that David and Harriet Raney built on Market Street in 1838. The Raney home is open to visitors on Saturdays.

The old lighthouse still stands on St. George Island; its beacon warns mariners of the dangerous shoals along the coast. The island is a shell-seeker's paradise.

Trinity Church, the Greek Revival building that was shipped from New York in four sections and assembled with wooden pegs in 1837–38, is on the National Register of Historical Places and is the second oldest church in Florida where services are still held. It stands as a permanent monument to glorify God for His bounteous goodness.

A Letter To Our Readers

Dear Reader:

In order that we might better contribute to your reading enjoyment, we would appreciate your taking a few minutes to respond to the following questions. We welcome your comments and read each form and letter we receive. When completed, please return to the following:

Rebecca Germany, Fiction Editor
Heartsong Presents
PO Box 719
Uhrichsville, Ohio 44683

1. Did you enjoy reading *Margaret's Quest?*
   ❑ Very much. I would like to see more books
     by this author!
   ❑ Moderately
     I would have enjoyed it more if _____

     _____

     _____

2. Are you a member of **Heartsong Presents**? Yes ❑ No ❑
   If no, where did you purchase this book? _____

   _____

3. How would you rate, on a scale from 1 (poor) to 5 (superior), the cover design? _____

4. On a scale from 1 (poor) to 10 (superior), please rate the following elements.

   _____ Heroine   _____ Plot

   _____ Hero   _____ Inspirational theme

   _____ Setting   _____ Secondary characters

5. These characters were special because_____

_____

_____

6. How has this book inspired your life?_____

_____

_____

7. What settings would you like to see covered in future **Heartsong Presents** books?_____

_____

_____

8. What are some inspirational themes you would like to see treated in future books?_____

_____

_____

9. Would you be interested in reading other **Heartsong Presents** titles?　　Yes ❑　　　　No ❑

10. Please check your age range:
    ❑ Under 18　　　❑ 18-24　　　❑ 25-34
    ❑ 35-45　　　　　❑ 46-55　　　❑ Over 55

11. How many hours per week do you read?_____

Name _____

Occupation _____

Address _____

City _____ State _____ Zip _____

Ah, those homemade,

comforting family dinners around the table. But who has time to make them between carpooling and softball games?

Don't let your busy schedule deter you. This collection of delectable recipes—from the readers and authors of inspirational romances—has been gathered from all over the United States, and even from Greece and Australia.

There are tried and true recipes for every occasion—Crock-Pot meals for busy days, fast desserts for church dinners, rave snacks for after school, holiday gifts for those picky relatives, and much, much more. Over 700 recipes await you! Bring back the joy of treasured moments over good food with the ones you love. So, dust off the china and treat your loved ones (and yourself) to some delicious home cooking.

The Heart's Delight *cookbook has what every family needs—cooking from the heart.*

400 pages, Paperbound, 8" x 5 ¾₁₆"

······ Hearts♥ng ······

Any 12 *Heartsong Presents* titles for only $26.95 *

*plus $1.00 shipping and handling per order and sales tax where applicable.

HISTORICAL ROMANCE IS CHEAPER BY THE DOZEN!

Buy any assortment of twelve *Heartsong Presents* titles and save 25% off of the already discounted price of $2.95 each!

·········· Presents ··········

_HP271 WHERE LEADS THE HEART, *Colleen Coble*

_HP272 ALBERT'S DESTINY, *Birdie L. Etchison*

_HP275 ALONG UNFAMILIAR PATHS, *Amy Rognlie*

_HP276 THE MOUNTAIN'S SON, *Gloria Brandt*

_HP279 AN UNEXPECTED LOVE, *Andrea Boeshaar*

_HP280 A LIGHT WITHIN, *Darlene Mindrup*

_HP283 IN LIZZY'S IMAGE, *Carolyn R. Scheidies*

_HP284 TEXAS HONOR, *Debra White Smith*

_HP287 THE HOUSE ON WINDRIDGE, *Tracie Peterson*

_HP288 SWEET SURRENDER, *JoAnn A. Grote*

_HP291 REHOBOTH, *DiAnn Mills*

_HP292 A CHILD OF PROMISE, *Jill Stengl*

_HP295 TEND THE LIGHT, *Susannah Hayden*

_HP296 ONCE MORE CHANCE, *Kimberley Comeaux*

_HP299 EM'S ONLY CHANCE, *Rosey Dow*

_HP300 CHANGES OF THE HEART, *Judith McCoy Miller*

_HP303 MAID OF HONOR, *Carolyn R. Scheidies*

_HP304 SONG OF THE CIMARRON, *Kelly R. Stevens*

_HP307 SILENT STRANGER, *Peggy Darty*

_HP308 A DIFFERENT KIND OF HEAVEN, *Tammy Shuttlesworth*

_HP311 IF THE PROSPECT PLEASES, *Sally Laity*

_HP312 OUT OF THE DARKNESS, *Dianna Crawford and Rachel Druten*

_HP315 MY ENEMY, MY LOVE, *Darlene Mindrup*

_HP316 FAITH IN THE GREAT SOUTHLAND, *Mary Hawkins*

_HP319 MARGARET'S QUEST, *Muncy Chapman*

_HP320 HOPE IN THE GREAT SOUTHLAND, *Mary Hawkins*

Great Inspirational Romance at a Great Price!

Heartsong Presents books are inspirational romances in contemporary and historical settings, designed to give you an enjoyable, spirit-lifting reading experience. You can choose wonderfully written titles from some of today's best authors like Peggy Darty, Sally Laity, Tracie Peterson, Colleen L. Reece, Lauraine Snelling, and many others.

When ordering quantities less than twelve, above titles are $2.95 each.
Not all titles may be available at time of order.

SEND TO: Heartsong Presents Reader's Service
P.O. Box 719, Uhrichsville, Ohio 44683

Please send me the items checked above. I am enclosing $_____.
(please add $1.00 to cover postage per order. OH add 6.25% tax. NJ add 6%). Send check or money order, no cash or C.O.D.s, please.
To place a credit card order, call 1-800-847-8270.

NAME _____

ADDRESS _____

CITY/STATE _____ ZIP _____

HPS 3-99